FORBIDDEN LUST

The Kingpin Series Book 1

BROOKE SUMMERS

Forbidden Lust
First Edition published in 2020

Cover Design by Lee Ching of Undercover Designs.
Formatter Kristine Moran of the Word Fairy.
Editing by Lisa Flynn of Simply Writing.
Proofread by Gemma Woolley of Gem's Precise Proofreads and by Nicole Wilson.

Created with Vellum

For you, for taking the time to read this story.

ONE

Mia

"Mia!" Sarah cries and I quickly pull on my strappy heels, throwing open the bathroom door I narrow my eyes as she claps her hands like a seal. "You look hot!" She smiles widely, "Are you planning on handing in your V-card tonight?"

I roll my eyes, that's all she's focused on. "No plans to." This has been a constant discussion between us in the last month, I haven't found anyone who I'm attracted to and I'm worried that there's something wrong with me.

She huffs at me as she flicks her blond hair over her shoulder, "Mia, you're going to college, no one goes to college as a virgin anymore."

"Shut up." I say as I throw my bag on the floor,

"I'm ready whenever you are." My nerves are setting in, I've never done anything like this before, if Mom knew what Sarah and I have planned she'd go crazy, she believes that I'm staying at Sarah's and Sarah's mom thinks she's staying with me tonight.

She claps her hands together and grins, "Let's go, I'm so excited. Tonight is going to be epic." She links her arm through mine and we walk out of the motel room and towards the BART station, four stops and we'll be in San Fran. My excitement is building as the adrenaline courses through my body.

Walking up to the club, there's a long line and I sigh, the longer we wait the more nervous I'm going to get, but Sarah grabs my hand and practically drags me toward the front of the line, causing a lot of groans from the people in the queue as we pass them and I instantly feel bad. I'd be pissed too if someone was cutting the line. "Hey Jagger." Sarah purrs as we come to a stop.

Jagger's at least six foot seven along with having tattoos snaking across his neck and when combined with his shaven head, gives him a menacing aura. He takes a sweeping glance at both Sarah and I, a smile spreading across his face. "Damn Sarah, looking good." He winks as he holds out his hands and we both pass him the fake IDs Sarah's brother Frankie got for us. He doesn't really pay much attention to them as his gaze is directed on Sarah's chest, he just hands them back to us, "Have a wonderful night ladies." He nods his head indicating for us to go on ahead.

Both Sarah and I casually stroll into the club, while inside I'm squealing. I can't believe we managed to get in. "Look a table, Mia, grab it and I'll get us some drinks." She instructs. My feet move toward the empty table and I take a sweeping glance around the club. It's crazy busy already, there's people talking and having fun while others are on the dance floor, the one thing they all have in common, is their bright smiles.

"Let's toast!" Sarah says loudly trying to be heard over the music as she hands me a drink. "To us, may we achieve everything we set our minds to. May we be happy wherever in this world we may end up, and lastly, may we forever be friends!" I raise my hand and our glasses clink against one another. "Mia, we've been friends since first grade, we've been through a lot and made it out the other end. Thank you for being here with me tonight."

Sarah and I have been friends since first grade, we along with six other girls had been inseparable since then. We'd do anything and everything together. We all had our weddings planned out, with the other seven girls being bridesmaids. That was up until two months ago when Sarah slept with Riley just after he had broken up with Lola. Yes, Sarah went against girl code but she didn't deserve the brutal shunning that all the girls gave her, I wouldn't be a part of that and I too was shunned. It showed me that they were never truly my friends if they could turn against me that quickly.

I give Sarah a warm smile, "I'm so glad that we came, I already feel lighter." I've been so stressed about going to college, it's going to be the furthest I've ever been away from home and I'm not sure if I'll be able to do it.

"Let's enjoy our last night together. Tomorrow is a new chapter." Sarah tells me. I'm going to miss her like crazy, she's going to New York to try and pursue a career in fashion. She wants to be anywhere but Oakland. She's happy to get away from the crap she's been dealing with.

"You want to dance?" She asks and I shake my head, I'm not in the mood yet. I'm not a great dancer and it takes it a while to gather the courage to let loose. "Suit yourself." She winks at me and leaves me at the table as she saunters off to the dance floor. Within seconds she's dancing with a guy, a beautiful smile on her face, she's so happy, it's good to see especially after her feeling down the past couple of months.

I stand here and watch silently as I sip on my drink. I can feel eyes on me, the heat from their gaze makes the hair on the back of my neck stand up. Turning around I can't see anyone in particular who's making me feel this way. Shaking my head I turn back to the dance floor. Sarah's having so much fun, she's really letting her hair down and relaxing. She smiles and waves over at me as the song changes and her eyes light up, its Cardi B's *Bodak Yellow* that fills the club, "Mia," She calls as she raises her arms in the air and her body begins to sway.

Downing the drink, I place the glass on the table and make my way over to Sarah, my hips swaying as I do so. Sarah reaches her hands out as I get closer to her and she pulls me toward her, both of us getting lost in the music and dancing away. Tonight, neither of us have any problems, we're living in the moment.

I manage to stay out dancing for six songs before I need a rest. Walking over to the bar, I order us Margaritas, I manage to get the table we were at when we first came in and place the two drinks down. Peering up at Sarah who's dancing alone, I've not seen her this happy for a long time, even before she slept with Riley.

A shadow falls over the table and I look up, and my breath catches as a gorgeous man stands before me. Jet black hair, piercing brown eyes and a smirk that screams bad boy, not to mention the tattoo that's peeking out from his shirt collar. "You alone?" His deep and gravely tone sends tingles down my spine. I instinctively know that he was the one who was staring at me earlier, the person who made the hair on my neck stand up.

My tongue sweeps across my bottom lip as I stare, mesmerized by him. I shake my head, "No, I'm here with a friend."

His eyebrow raises in question, "Friend?"

"Yeah, friend." I tell him and I glance over at Sarah, she's now dancing with the guy she had danced with earlier.

His lips twitch, "That's good."

"Oh and why is that?" I ask, my voice husky. I can't believe that I'm flirting with this guy. I've never flirted with anyone, I'm usually the shy one, the girl that gets overlooked because my friends are amazing.

"Because you're coming home with me tonight and I'd hate to break up a relationship."

I splutter, "I'm sorry, says who?" How dare he?

"Says me." He smiles and God, he's beautiful.

"I'll think about it." I don't know what the hell has gotten into me tonight but I'm tempted to go home with him.

His smile widens, "You do that." He slowly walks away, his eyes boring into me as he does so. I can't take my eyes off of him.

"Who's the hunk?" I spin on my seat, my heart beating fast as I come face to face with Sarah, her eyes on the crowd that the guy just disappeared into.

Taking a sip of my drink, trying to steady the rhythm of my pulse. The tequila is strong but the lime takes the edge off of it. "I don't know."

"So, are you going home with him?"

I gape at her, "How the hell did you hear that?"

She shrugs, "I didn't, I can lip read. You should totally do it."

“I don’t know, I don’t even know his name. Hell he just asked if I was alone and then told me that I was going home with him.” What the hell has gotten into me? I would think that was an ultimate turnoff and yet, I find it sexy as hell.

Her eyes widen and a slow smirk forms on her lips, "That is hot! Look, see how you feel by the end of the night. You can go with him and see where it takes you. No one is pressuring you to do anything, if they do, I'll kick their ass." She winks at me as she picks the Margarita up and takes a sip, "He really is hot."

I nod, "Yeah he is." He's freaking gorgeous. "What about you? You going home with that guy?"

She waves her hand dismissively, "I'm not sure, we're just dancing at the moment. I'd love to go home with Jagger, but I don't see that happening."

"Why?"

She tips her chin behind me and I turn and see Jagger standing by the door, his arm around some girl's waist as they talk. "That's why. She's Carina, she's his on and off again girlfriend. The last I heard they were off permanently. Guess that's no longer the case."

Shit, gone is her happiness and in its place is the usual defeated, sad Sarah that I'm used to seeing. "His loss, come on, let's go and dance again."

We both finish our drinks and she smiles, "You're right. It's his loss. Besides, it's not as though I'm going to see him again after tomorrow so what's the point?"

Linking my arm through hers we make our way to the dance floor, the hairs on the back of my neck stand up once again, turning I see the dark-haired sexy God standing at the back of the club with his arms crossed looking at Sarah and I. My heart begins to race as his eyes rake over my body.

"Mia, I've never seen you so flustered before." Sarah says as we dance, "You keep glancing at the back of the club, is he there?"

"Yes, he hasn't taken his eyes off of us."

She scoffs, "Oh Mia, my sweet, sweet Mia. His eyes are not on me."

"What am I going to do Sarah?" This is all so new to me, I've no idea what to do, and I don't even know what to say or how to act. I should forget it and go back to the motel with Sarah.

"Mia, that's something I can't tell you. What does your head tell you?"

I laugh, "To run back to the motel."

She smiles, "And your heart?"

I throw my head back and groan, "My heart wants to go and see what happens."

She pulls me into her arms, "Your head wants to protect your heart, and you have to decide which one you want to follow."

I nod, "I guess it's going to be a decision I make when the time comes."

"That time is going to come sooner than you realize." She laughs, "Mia, it's almost closing."

Glancing around the club, the throbbing crowd from earlier is thinning, I catch sight of a guy holding his girl's shoes as they leave the club hand in hand. A cheer rings out, turning, I see a guy downing his beer being egged on by his friends. Damn, she's right. "One more drink?" It may help me make a decision.

She shrugs, "Yeah sure, we are celebrating after all."

Fifteen minutes later and the club is closing, I glance around and see that the mystery man is gone. That makes up my mind anyway. Sarah isn't leaving with anyone either. I'm not upset; I've actually had an amazing night.

"Ladies." A deep voice says as we reach the door.

I turn around and see Jagger standing there waiting for us, "Hey," I say softly, but he doesn't respond, his eyes darkening as they take in Sarah.

"Hey Jagger, did you have a good night?" She asks softly, a flirty smile on her lips.

His tongue darts out and swipes at his bottom

lip. "I'm hoping it's about to get a hell of a lot better, sweetness. You want to come back to my place?"

Sarah instantly nods, and I suck in a sharp breath. Damn, what is with these men and the way they can make us lose our minds? "Jag," Sarah says turning to face him, her brow furrowed, "Do you know her mystery man?"

A cocky grin appears on his face, "Describe him. I know a lot of people."

"Tall, jet black hair, piercing brown eyes." Heat rises in my cheeks as I describe him. "He has a tattoo on his neck."

"Sugar," He says a bright smile on his face, "take a seat and wait a moment, your man's coming for you." The last couple of party goers leave, making us the only ones left here. Sarah walks up to Jagger, and he wastes no time in wrapping his arms around her. I have to look away as they make gooey eyes at each other. "He's a good man, he'll treat you right." He tells me, and I feel a little less anxious about staying here.

Sarah rushes over to me, "Remember what I said, do whatever you want, today is our last day here Mia, I want it to be one we remember. Meet me back at the motel at six, that way we'll be home and no one will notice."

"Okay, have fun," I whisper to her, nerves and excitement starting to settle in me. He didn't leave, he's still here. I'm really tempted to go back with him and see where this goes.

Her smile is infectious, "Oh, trust me, I will." Jagger pulls his keys out of his pocket and takes a step toward the exit. Sarah looks back at me, hesitates and places a hand on Jagger's chest to stop him. "Do you want us to wait with you?"

I shake my head, "No, you two go and have fun."

"I'll see you tomorrow," Sarah calls out as they leave, Jagger locking up behind him, leaving me alone in this club.

I take out my cell from the hidden pocket in my dress; there are no missed calls or texts. I'm not sure why I thought there would be, Mom has no reason to believe I'm not at Sarah's house. I've been there a million times before.

I quickly send a message to Sarah's brother, Frankie. He's like my brother too; he's been a part of my life for a long time. I've not seen much of him since he joined the Military. He's a SEAL, and a good one at that.

Be safe out there and come home to us.

I'm going to miss him, but I'm proud of him, he's doing what he's wanted to do since he was a teenager. He replies instantly.

You know me, nothing can bring me down.

I shake my head, he's such an ass.

Frankie I'm being serious. Be safe.

His reply makes me sad as I don't know when the next time we'll see each other will be.

Always Mia, look after yourself and I'll see you soon.

Putting my cell back in my pocket, I glance around the club, it's completely empty and looks so different than when it's open. The bar is black and when the main lights are on it looks fluorescent. It's such a cool feature, but makes it look ordinary once the lights aren't on.

Hands run down my arms, leaving goosebumps in their wake. "Sorry for the delay." His deep voice settles over me, making my heart race. "Thank you for waiting."

I turn to face him. It's weird being the only ones left in the club. "No worries," I reply softly, unsure of myself and what I'm doing here.

His hand comes up to my chin, and his fingers

tilt my face up so that I'm looking into those gorgeous brown eyes of his, I could get lost in them, "Do you want to come with me?"

My tongue darts out and licks my bottom lip, I'm nervous, and it's showing. "Yes. I want to come with you."

He leans down, and his mouth captures mine. This isn't soft and sweet like I thought it would be, it's hard and consuming. Our lips are closed, but it doesn't matter. It's still the best kiss I've ever had and if this is a preview of what's to come then sign me up. "Ready?" He asks as he pulls away from me.

I nod, I'm unable to talk, he's left me breathless.

"Good." He smirks and helps me to my feet. His hand on the base of my back, he leads us to the door which he unlocks and then leads me out of the club. The fresh air fills my lungs as I wait for him to lock the club up, when he's finished he leads me into a waiting car. Shit, he has a chauffeur. Climbing into the back, he gets in beside me, and his hand grips my thigh. His fingers begin to slowly caress my leg. Heat rises throughout my body, and I squeeze my legs together as liquid pools there. Shit, I've never been so turned on from someone touching me before. Leaning closer, his lips graze the outer shell of my ear. "I can't wait to get you inside my house. I can't wait to finally have you, watching you all night has been driving me crazy." He whispers, and I whimper. "We're going to have fun tonight."

I don't know how much time passes before we reach his house, but it only seems like minutes. He's been driving me crazy the entire drive, his fingers caressing my skin, going higher and higher up my leg but never going anywhere near my panties. His breath hot against my ear as he whispered what he wanted to do to me when he got me inside. He helps me out of the car, placing his hand on the base of my back. I'm hot and bothered, I need him, and I have no idea how or why, but I know that I do.

As soon as we enter the house, he's on me. His mouth fusing against mine, his tongue sweeping into my mouth and our teeth clashing. It's hot, wild, and brutal. It's amazing. My hands go to his shirt, wanting, no *needing* to touch him. "The first time is going to be quick. I hope you didn't plan on getting any sleep tonight. I have plans for you." He growls as he pulls my dress over my head, leaving me standing in my panties and heels. His eyes darken as he rakes over my body. "I'm going to have so much fun with you."

TWO

Hudson

"Boss, we've got a problem." Jagger's southern drawl comes over the line.

"What?" I ask. It's almost ten, and I've just sat down in my office. That fucking bitch Carina texted me asking me if she can have an advance. She's crazy, I'm not her man, and she doesn't work for me, I don't owe her shit, and yet she has the cheek to ask me to give her drugs without paying. In her fucking dreams.

"Kane's body has been found." He tells me, peering at the camera outside, he's in the shadows, away from the crowd of people waiting to get in. Jagger's my bouncer along with being my right-hand man.

I shake my head. He's been missing for two

days. I knew he was dead; there's no way he'd go that long without checking in. "What happened?"

"Bullet between the eyes." He says matter-of-factly.

This is a message, whoever shot him wanted to send a message. I've received it loud and clear. They're not going to get away with this. You don't execute my men and live to tell the tale.

"Find out who did it!"

"Boss, I already know. It was Healy."

"Why the fuck are those Irish gangsters killing my men?" They've crossed the line. We didn't have any problems until now.

"Seems as though Kane was playing around with Healy's daughter…" There's a pause, Jagger's fucking pissed. "Boss, she's sixteen." He bites out.

Fuck, I would have killed Kane myself, that asshole was twenty-nine, you don't do that shit with a sixteen-year-old.

"I'll call Healy and see what the fuck is up." He should have come to me. I would have dealt with Kane. "Make sure Carina stays the hell away from my club tonight Jagger. I'm sick of dealing with her pathetic ass. We're not a charity, I don't give anything away for free."

His sigh is heavy, "She still at that crap? Don't worry Boss, I'll make sure that she doesn't show up."

"Good, I don't want her stepping foot in the club, she's bad for business." She's a mess. That woman's so high she could be a damn kite. "It's time you got rid of her Jag."

He's silent for a beat. "Are you demanding I get rid of her?"

I grind my teeth together. I wish I could tell him to, but I'm not a prick. Well, not all the time. "No, it's your life, do as you please. I'm telling you as a friend that she's toxic."

"I know you don't like her Hudson, but trust me, I know what I'm doing." This is the same speech he's been giving me for almost two years now.

"If you say so. I'll talk to you later. I have Healy to deal with." I tell him and hang up.

I scroll through my cell until I come to John Healy's name. Hitting call, I grit my teeth as I listen to it ring. My hand is shaking with rage the longer I wait for him to answer.

"I've been waiting for this call," John says as he answers.

"John, *you* should have fucking called *me*," I say through gritted teeth.

He sighs, "I was planning to, but as soon as JJ found out what that piece of shit had been doing to his sister, all politeness left. I had to make a call: be with my son while he dealt with the fuck who defiled his little sister, or give you a courtesy call."

I'm silent as I let what he's just said digest. What would I have done if I were in his shoes?

"Look, Hudson, I respect you a hell of a lot more than I do your old man and I'll respect whatever decision you make in regards to what's going to happen to us. If the shoe was on the other foot, I wouldn't even hesitate."

"How many people know what happened?" I ask. I've already made my decision.

"My family and obviously your men." He replies instantly, confusion in his voice.

"How many know you didn't talk to me beforehand?"

"None, I've not said anything, and JJ has asked, but I told him to mind his damn business. Hudson, what the hell are you thinking?" He snaps. Like me, he hates games and even though I'm not playing one, I *am* holding out on him.

"It was sanctioned. I gave you the go-ahead after you came to me." This could go fucking south, but if it does, I'll slaughter the lot of them. "Betray me John, and I'll unleash holy hell on you and your family."

"I wouldn't Hudson, how long have I known you? When have I ever given you the impression that I'd do that?" He's right. He's never done anything for me to believe he'd betray me. I don't trust him, not fully, but I do consider him a close ally. "I owe you, and big time. You need me, call. I don't care what it's for. Understand?"

"I understand John. I'll talk to you soon."

"Thank you Hudson, you're a good man." He tells me and hangs up, leaving me to laugh. I'm not a good man, I'm the son of the drug and gun kingpin. We're the biggest supplier on the west coast. If I were in charge, I'd change up the whole fucking organization.

Having me say I gave the go-ahead for Kane's murder could mean a lot of crap for me to deal with. Everything is meant to go through Dad. My boys call me Boss as I'm *their* boss, but I still have to answer to *my* boss... My dad. He's going to have something to fucking say about this, but I couldn't give a fuck. I'll be taking over one day, and when I do, I'll be doing things a hell of a lot differently.

"Boss," Barney growls, opening the door and walking into my office, without even asking. "Matt and Carmine. They're fucking morons." He's pissed because he's having to babysit them tonight.

"What have they done now?" I don't move my focus from the screen in front of me as I watch a young man move from person to person an easy smile on his face as he greets them all with a handshake. I shake my head, seeing the birthday pin on his top. He's celebrating his twenty-first. "They're in a fucking strip club right now, drunk as skunks. I'm not a babysitter, why the hell should I have to watch their asses?"

I sigh, "You fucked up Barney, you almost started a war with Antonio Conte. Dad's pissed so until someone else fucks up and he has someone else to hate, you're on the shit jobs."

"His sister's hot, all three of them. I don't understand what the fuss is about? She was as willing as I was." He has a big smile on his face, he damn well knows what the problem is.

"Get out of my office, and do some damn work," I tell him, as I glance once more at the screen before my eyes narrow in on a woman standing at a table; long raven hair, strappy shoes, legs that go on for miles. Her ass is barely covered in the tight, light pink dress she's wearing. She's got curves that have my dick stirring.

"Something interesting Boss?" Barney quips and I fire him a look, one that has him scurrying for the door.

Glancing back at the screen, she's with a blonde woman, and no man seems to be around them. I get up out of my chair and make my way onto the club floor. I stand at the bar, hidden by the crowds of people, but I'm able to see her. She turns almost as if she's able to feel my stare. Holy shit, she's fucking beautiful. She shakes her head and turns back to look out onto the dance floor. I'm unable to take my eyes off her.

"Hey Hudson," that whiny fake voice sets my teeth on edge, I don't turn to face her, however. I scan the crowd to look for Jagger. He needs to remove her ass from my club.

Her hand touches my shoulder, and I shrug her off, "Don't fucking touch me." I bite out as I glare at her. Her make up is all over the place, are those fake eyelashes? Why the hell are they falling off? Her tits are practically falling out of her dress. I roll my eyes. She really is a disaster. "What are you doing here Carina?"

She glares right back at me, she has no respect. "I wanted to talk to you. You didn't respond to my message."

I get in her face, "Get your skanky ass out of my club. I'm not your dealer, I don't give freebies. Get yourself cleaned up. You look a fucking state."

"How dare you?" She screams, her face getting red with rage.

"My bad, Boss," Jagger says as his arm goes around her waist and he drags her away.

I stare at the fucking moron as he pulls her into a corner and they talk. He really needs to get rid of her.

I glance back toward the table the woman was at and see she's gone. Her glass is still there so she mustn't have left the club. I search for her friend on the dance floor, they're dancing together, looking as though they don't have a care in the world. She makes her way to the bar after a couple of songs, she's in her own world. She doesn't even notice the appreciative looks she's getting from the men in the club. She makes her way back to the table. This is my opportunity to introduce myself.

She takes a sip from her cocktail. The salt around the rim of the glass tells me it's a Margarita. I wait until she places her drink down before walking over to her. She glances up at me as I reach the table. Her fucking eyes are magnificent, emerald green. "You alone?" I watch as she shivers. I already know that she's with her friend.

Her tongue peeks out and sweeps across her bottom lip as she stares at me, I can picture her licking my dick from base to tip. She shakes her head, "No, I'm here with a friend."

My eyebrows raise in question, "Friend?" Are they waiting for their men to join them?

"Yeah, friend." She glances at her friend on the dance floor, before turning back to face me, her cheeks a slight shade of pink, damn she's cute.

I fight the urge to smile, "That's good."

"Oh, and why is that?" Holy fuck, her voice is husky, and I want her to say my name with that tone. Shit, my dick's straining against my suit pants. Begging to be freed.

"Because you're coming home with me tonight and I'd hate to break up a relationship," I tell her and watch as what I've just said registers with her.

She splutters, "I'm sorry, says who?"

"Says me." I smile. I like her. I want her in my bed.

"I'll think about it." She says and not in a way to appease me. She's actually going to think about that.

That only makes me smile harder, "You do that." Her eyes on me as I walk away.

A couple of hours later and the club's closed. I've just finished cashing up and sorting everything out. My mystery woman is waiting for me by the bar, and I'm pleased that she hasn't left. I wasn't sure if she would stay or not. But damn, now that she has, I'm going to have a fucking good night. I need to get her to my house and get inside of her. There's something about her that's calling to me, I've been instantly attracted to a girl before, but this, this is different.

Walking out of the club, Martin's waiting at the curb for us, he doesn't say anything when she climbs into the back of the car, her dress riding up her thighs just a little. My hand reaches out, needing to touch her. I gently caress her thigh and her skin is smooth against my calloused hand, "I can't wait to get you inside my house. I can't wait to finally have you. Watching you all night has been driving me crazy." I lean in and whisper, she whimpers, and that sound makes me hard again. "We're going to have fun tonight."

My fingers caress her thighs the entire car ride, I've been driving myself fucking crazy touching her, but I know that she's uneasy by the way she keeps glancing at me, her eyes filled with uncertainty. But as soon as I turn my focus onto her she eases. Martin finally pulls up outside my house, and I'm out of the car before he's even switched the engine off. I help her out of the car, my hand going to her back as I lead her to the house.

As soon as I close the door, I'm on her like a starved man. My tongue delves into her mouth, and I take everything she's offering, those tiny whimpers of hers tell me how much she's loving this. "The first time is going to be quick. I hope you didn't plan on getting any sleep tonight. I have plans for you." I growl as I pull her dress off over her head. She's standing in front of me in her underwear, fuck she's beautiful. "I'm going to have so much fun with you."

I pull off her panties, and her pussy is exposed to me. She tries to hide herself, but I stop her, pulling her hands away. "Show me." My voice is gruffer than I've ever heard it. "I'm going to eat that pussy later, but right now, my dick needs feeding," I tell her and watch as her eyes widen as I set my dick free from my pants.

"Are you ready for this?" I ask her. She's standing there like a doe caught in the headlights.

Her tongue peeks out of her mouth again, and she wets her lips. "Yes." She whispers.

My hands immediately go to her hips, her skin like porcelain, delicate and soft. I lift her up and pin her to the wall, her legs wrap around my waist as her hands grip my neck. My lips descend on hers as I line her pussy up with my dick. As soon as I inch my way inside of her, the walls of her pussy clench. Fuck! She's tight, God, this is perfect. I take my time and inch slower into her, before withdrawing and doing it again, I've only moved a slight bit inside her.

She whimpers, her fingernails digging into the skin around my neck. I can't take it anymore. I need to be sated, deep inside her. Pulling out of her once more, I thrust all the way inside of her. She screams out in pain as I break past the barrier, and I still. What. The. Fuck? She's a virgin? How? Why? Shit. I can't contemplate that right now as I'm dying to move, I'm buried inside the tightest pussy I've ever been in, and I need to move, but I can't hurt her. I won't hurt her. I've never been with a virgin before and fuck it feels good.

I move a bit and see that she's not wincing in

pain, I do it again this time pulling out and thrusting gently inside of her. She moans, her legs tightening around me. Oh, yeah. She's enjoying this now. "You okay?" I ask, and she nods, whimpering as I slide into her again.

"Harder?" I need to make sure she's okay with it.

"Yes, oh please, do something." She cries, and I do. I slam back into her and her hands grip my hair, I lose control completely, thrusting in and out of her like a mad man. I'm possessed, and I have no idea why. She's got me fucked up, and I don't care.

"I'm going to come," I tell her as I feel the orgasm building.

"Do it." She breathes in my ear and I thrust a few more times before exploding inside of her.

"Next time, you're going to come," I promise her when I recover and am able to breathe. I carry her to my bedroom and lay her on the bed. "Let me take care of your pussy first," I say as I get down on my knees and open her up for me, damn, she's red and puffy. I fucked her too hard for her first time.

"No, it's okay." She says, trying to push me off.

"Did you like what we just did?"

She stills, "Yes."

"Then trust me, you're going to love this," I

promise her, and I get to work, showing her just how great oral sex is.

Turning over, I feel emptiness. Opening my eyes, the bed is empty. Sitting up, I realize the house is quiet. Shit, she's gone. I reach for my cell and see that it's eight am, fuck. I hit dial on Jagger's number.

"It's early. This had better be good." He gripes.

"Is your girl gone?" I know he went home with my girl's friend. Anyone's better than fucking Carina.

"What?" He asks, and I realize I've just woke him up. "Shit. How did you know?"

"Mine has gone too. Jag, find them." I demand and hang up. I instantly call Martin. "Martin, find that woman who I left the bar with last night. I don't care how you do it. Just do it." I hang up without letting him answer. I'm like a fucking mad man, I had one night with the woman, and I'm desperate to see her again. Fuck, that's not right.

My men had better find her; otherwise, I'm going to go crazy. I throw my phone, and it bounces off the wall, smashing into pieces. Why did she leave? Where the hell has she gone? I wasn't finished with her yet. "You can run Princess, but you can't hide. I'm going to find you, and when I do, I'm going to make you mine." I whisper. It's a promise. She's never getting away from me again.

THREE

Mia

Twenty Months later

Ugh, I'm dreading the drive home. It's summer break, and I've been summoned to return home.

"Mia, are you sure it's okay that I tag along too?" Lacey asks as she stands by my bedroom door, "I mean you're meeting your stepdad for the first time." Her parents are in the Bahamas this summer and she'd be home alone if she went back to Carson City.

I throw her a smirk, "I've spoken to Mom, she's expecting you. Apparently, her and daddy dearest are throwing a party." I roll my eyes. It sounds so pretentious and something that my mom would never do. I guess a lot of things have changed since she married Harrison Brady. They eloped two weeks ago. I only found out that they were married once they returned.

She perks up, "A party?" She doesn't really go to parties here, I think because I'm her only friend here in Arizona, she's so shy around everyone at college and yet with me, she's herself and I love her as if she were my sister, so hearing her perk up at the mention of a party surprises me.

I nod, "Yeah, it's probably going to be filled with old men and women who Mom and Harrison are going to show off to." Mom is selling our old house. The one that Dad took years saving for, the one that his life insurance paid for. She's moved into some other house, she's sent me pictures and has even picked out a room for me to have. No matter what, that house will never be home.

Lacey walks into my room, "I know that you're mad Mia, but your mom seems really happy." She puts her arm around my shoulders and pulls me into her body, "You should try and forgive her for not telling you and be happy for her."

I sigh, "I am happy for her, I just feel as though she's getting rid of any memory of Dad while she moves on. It's like she's forgotten him." My dad died five years ago from a brain aneurism. He served twenty years in the army only to retire and die anyway. It hurt, and I'm mad that my mom's trying to wipe him from her memory, remove all remnants of their life together. Am I next?

Lacey pulls away from me, "It's a good thing that I'll be there with you every step of the way. I'd better finish packing." She begins to walk out of my room.

"We'll leave in an hour, so be ready," I yell out and hear her grunt in acknowledgment.

Grabbing my phone off the bed, I call Mom to let her know that we'll be leaving soon.

She answers on the second ring. "Hey baby, have you left yet?"

"Not yet, we're just finishing packing up. We'll be leaving here in an hour," I tell her as I throw more clothes haphazardly into the bag. "I'm almost packed and Lacey's just finishing off too."

"That's good baby. I can't wait to see you. It's been too long."

I don't tell her that's her own fault, "I'll be there soon, Mom. What's the plan for this evening?" I know my mom, she likes to have plans, she makes lists too.

"I want you and Harrison to get to know one and other, so we'll be having dinner. It'll just be the four of us as Harrison's son won't be arriving until the morning." Her voice rises a pitch, and she's talking a mile a minute. Guilt sets in for being so angry at her.

"Okay, I'll text you when we're leaving. It shouldn't be too long. I don't want to be driving when it's dark. Love you, Mom, bye."

"Love you too, baby, drive safe, and I'll see you soon."

I end the call and throw my phone back onto the bed and continue to throw everything and anything into my suitcase. I don't know why I'm bothering as I've got a closet full of clothes at Mom's. "Hey Lacey, you need any help?" I yell as I grab my phone and my bag and walk out of my room and toward the kitchen.

"No, I'm good. I'm almost ready." She yells back, "I just need to grab my toothbrush." She's so weird. I always have a new toothbrush when I'm traveling anywhere.

I grab my car keys off the kitchen counter, "We'll leave as soon as you're ready and stop somewhere for some food. I'm starving." I shout as I open the front door, I notice my ASU hoodie on the back of the couch and grab it, it's one of the most comfortable hoodies I own, and I love wearing it while lounging around the house.

Her laughter follows me out of the house, "When aren't you?" Looking over my shoulder, I see her walking out of the house, her bag in her hand and a smile on her face. "But I agree, we should stop and get something to eat and use a restroom."

I laugh, "Any road trip we take, you need to pee every five minutes."

She shrugs, throwing her bag into the trunk of the car, "I get excited." She laughs.

"Like a dog."

She gapes, "Hey!" But she can't keep a straight enough face to fake outrage.

I stick my tongue out at her and walk past her back into the house. "Have you got everything?" I don't need to look back to see her rolling her eyes, "Don't roll your eyes at me, missy." I mock.

"Yes, Mom. I'm ready whenever you are." I hear the car door close, and I know that she'll be racing into the house in a few seconds so that she can go to the bathroom again.

I fill up the travel mugs so that we'll be fueled up and grab the bag of snacks I got ready earlier. Lacey and I love junk food. I'm crazy on candies whereas Lacey loves chips. We eat ourselves sick when we take road trips, but it's fun, and now it's our tradition.

"I need to pee," Lacey yells running past the kitchen and toward the bathroom.

"Hurry up, or I'm leaving without you." I take the bag of snacks along with the coffee cups and make my way to the door, "Will you please lock up?" I ask and wait for her grunt before going to the car. Thankfully Lacey left the passenger's side door open, so I place the coffee mugs on her seat and walk around to the driver's side and get in.

Turning the engine on, I quickly reach for the volume as *'Living on a Prayer'* by Bon Jovi comes on and nearly blows my eardrums, I always forget to turn down the music before I get out of the car. A bang has me looking in the mirror to see Lacey locking the door. I quickly send Mom a text, letting her know that we're about to leave.

"Okay ready this time." She huffs as she climbs into the car.

"You sure?"

She slaps my shoulder, "Yes, now let's get going before I need to pee again."

I put the car into drive and glance at her, "You

need to see a doctor about that." I smirk as I pull out of the driveway and onto the street.

"No I don't, it just happens whenever we go on a road trip. I get excited."

I snicker, "Then see a vet."

"Har-har, funny. So how much do you know about your new family?" She uses her fingers to make quotation marks as she says family.

"I don't really know much about them, why?"

She makes a weird noise, and I glance at her. She's looking down at her hands, "What?"

"Your new brother is Hudson *Brady*, Mia."

I shake my head, "And he is?" Up until Mom married Harrison, I had never heard of Hudson.

She sits forward, her hands clasping her knees as she brings her feet up onto the seat. "Mia, Hudson's dangerous. I've heard things about him, nothing good."

I frown, "What do you mean dangerous?"

She's silent, and it freaks me out. She obviously knows about him; otherwise she wouldn't have mentioned it. "Lacey?"

She sighs, "Look, I personally don't know him, but when Greg heard me mention your stepdad, Harrison, he asked if your new brother was called

Hudson. When I told him it was, he told me things."

I press my foot against the break as we come to a stop sign, once the car has fully come to a stop, I turn and look at her, "Told you what?"

She holds her hands up in surrender, "Greg said that Hudson's involved in some pretty shady things."

I roll my eyes, this sounds like bullshit, "Oh yeah, like what exactly?" I ask as I put the car into drive again.

"Guns, drugs, and anything that you shouldn't be doing, he does. Greg said that Hudson's some sort of boss or something like that. Although it's all hearsay, no one actually knows for sure."

"Okaaayyy and I'm a fairy princess." I laugh, "Lacey, Hudson's twenty-seven, do you really think they let men at that age be bosses of organized crime?"

She claps her hands, "See, that's exactly what I said. Most of those bosses are like old, in their sixties or something like that."

"We watch way too many crime dramas, but yeah, I think Greg's full of shit. Anyway, we'll meet him tomorrow morning, he won't be attending dinner." I'm intrigued, I want to find out more about him. Mom's not really told me much other than he's twenty-seven and he lives in San Francisco whereas Mom and Harrison live in the Hidden Hills. A far cry from where we used to live in Oakland. It's been a while since I've been back to Cali, so much has changed since I've been there. Hell, I'm not even going to Oakland.

"He's probably out killing people." Lacey laughs at her own joke, "Are we staying at your mom's the entire evening?"

I shake my head, she loves a good party, "I'm not sure, I'm not real hip with the Hidden Hills people and where they like to party. If things go south at dinner, we can always go to Oakland."

"We'll see where the night takes us." She replies, you'd think she was a hippy with the crap she comes out with sometimes, but she's not, she's just happy to get her buzz on wherever and whenever she can.

"Oh look, an IHOP, fancy a late breakfast?" I ask her, wanting pancakes. We're ten hours away from Cali, and we're only an hour into our trip. No doubt we'll stop at least twice more. But it's the fun of having a road trip.

Lacey moans, "Pancakes." We're both crap cooks, so we usually eat Ramen noodles or PB and J sandwiches. We rarely eat take-out either, so when we do we eat loads.

I pull into the parking lot and Lacey's climbing out of the car before I've even turned the ignition off. I shake my head, she loves her food, or she needs to pee again.

"This can't be right?" I say to Lacey as we pull up outside a fancy house, I knew the Hidden Hills was full of huge houses, but damn this is something else. It's huge. When Mom told me she'd moved into a new house, this isn't what I had envisioned. This must-have cost a bomb.

"The directions your mom gave say this is the right place." Her eyes are wide and full of awe, I'd say much like mine are. "Mia, God, this house is freaking huge!"

"Huge? It's humongous." It's bigger than any house I've ever seen before. It has black iron gates that hide it away from the outside world, so much glass. The windows look as if they go floor to ceiling. It's beautiful. My mouth's open wide as I just stare at it, this place must have cost a fortune, money that I know my mom doesn't have. I feel very uncomfortable with the fact I'll be staying somewhere so extravagant.

The gates begin to open, and I turn my gaze to Lacey, "Ready?" My pulse racing, I'm nervous and yet excited to see what this place is like but also to see my mom.

Her face breaks out into an enormous smile, "Am I ever, my heart's pounding with anticipation. I'm so glad that you invited me to come with you."

I laugh as I pull into the driveway, "You shouldn't thank me just yet, we've only just got here. This could end disastrously."

"I must make sure I have popcorn if it does."

I park my car in the driveway and get out of the car, hearing the gates closing, peering down, I gasp. The view is amazingly beautiful. We're so far up in the hills that we can see for miles. Mom must love it here.

"Mia." I hear the softness of my mom's voice, and I glance to the door to see her standing there with a beautiful smile on her face. She's decked head to toe in black. She looks stunning, yet expensive. Before Harrison, Mom would dress in whatever she could afford, right now she looks like she walked straight off a runway.

"Hey, Mom." I say as she wraps her arms around me, "You look beautiful."

Her arms tighten around me, "Thank you, Mia, it must be where you get it from." We both laugh, "It's good to have you home." She whispers as she releases me,

"Lacey," Mom says as Lacey walks up to us, she doesn't hesitate to also pull Lacey into her arms to give her a hug.

"Hey, Mrs. Brady." Lacey says returning the hug, "Mia's right, you look beautiful."

Mom steps back and smirks at us both, "So how much crap did you eat on the way here?"

Lacey and I glance at each other, "I have no idea what you're talking about." I tell her with a straight face, if anyone looked in my car they'd know we stopped off at most gas stations along the way and refueled with anything and everything.

"Mrs. Brady, we're having a wonderful dinner this evening, would we ruin that by eating crap?" Lacey goes overboard with the lie, her lips twitch with a barely concealed smile.

Mom laughs as she shakes her head, "You two are as bad as each other, I don't know which one of you is the bad influence."

"She is." We both say as we point at each other.

Mom just shakes her head, "You two." She says, before turning to walk into the house, "Come on, let's get you inside, and I can show you to your rooms."

I gasp when I reach the front door and catch a glimpse of the inside. Classy. It's the only way that I can describe it. The floor to ceiling windows add so much light to the hall, and it's a huge hall at that, dominated by a marble staircase. The walls are white, and the tiled floor is white with a few black lines per tile, it looks amazing, and I'm worried about staying here in case I break something.

"Mom, holy shit." I breathe in awe, turning to look at her.

Her eyes light up in happiness, "This is my dream house. I'm so fortunate to have it." Her voice soft, but her smile is bright and radiant. She's happier than I have ever seen her. "Come on, I'll show you to your rooms, and you can explore the house later." She takes my hand and leads me toward the stairs. "Lacey, you'll be on this floor with Harrison and I, if that's okay?"

I turn and look at Lacey, her eyes wide as she takes in everything around her, "Of course Mrs. Brady, I'd have been happy with the sofa."

"That would never happen Lacey." She says as

we walk up the stairs, "You're just here on our left." Mom says as she reaches the door.

"Thank you." Lacey replies softly as she opens the door and gasps, "This is bigger than our entire house."

I peer into the room and see that she's right, it *is* bigger than our house in Arizona. There's a king-sized bed, and like the hall, it's white, even the bedding is white. As I take a step inside the room, I see the floral print on the other wall. It looks phenomenal, and it's so Mom.

"Mrs. Brady, this is awesome." Lacey has a smile as big as Mom's. "Can I move in permanently?"

Mom laughs, "Want to see Mia's room?" She asks, and I glance at Lacey. We're both wondering what it's going to look like. "Once Hudson arrives, he'll be on the same floor as you, I want you both to get along, I know he's quite a bit older than you, but he's your brother now."

I roll my eyes, "He's hardly my brother, Mom." I'm excited to meet him, but I don't want to be forced to spend time with him while I'm here, what if we don't like each other? That would be so awkward.

"Just try and be nice." She warns me as we walk up another flight of stairs, whoever decorated this house sure loved the color white. It's everywhere, each and every wall has white on it, not to mention the marble staircase along with the tiles. I'd be surprised if there was a room that didn't have white in it.

"Okay," Mom begins, and I watch as excitement grows in her eyes. "So, I wanted you to feel at home here." She seems nervous.

I frown, "Okay, Mom."

She opens the door to a room, and I'm speechless, it's not white, it's a deep maroon color. The room is bigger than Lacey's, and that's something I didn't think could be possible. There's a sofa in the corner and beside it is a small bookcase. Walking into the room, I walk over to the bookcase and run my fingers across the spines of the books that are there. Mom went all out. She bought books from my favorite authors. Nora Roberts, Harper Sloan, Carly Phillips, and of course E.L. James. I love the story of Christian and Ana, it's such a beautiful love story.

"Thanks Mom," I whisper, tears stinging in my eyes, she's so thoughtful with the little things she's added to my room.

"I just want you to feel at home here Mia," She gently strokes my hair, "I miss you so much," she whispers, she sounds as though she's going to cry. "I'll let you two get sorted. Dinner will be ready in a couple of hours. So no rush."

"Thanks Mom."

"Thanks, Mrs. Brady."

Lacey and I say at the same time, I stick my tongue out at Lacey, and she returns by sticking her middle finger up at me while making sure that Mom can't see her.

"I'll call you when it's ready," Mom tells us, giving me another hug. "I'm glad you're here." She whispers before walking out of my room leaving Lacey and I alone.

"Holy shit Mia, this place is awesome. I can't wait to explore and see what else is here."

I nod, "Me too, but first let's grab our bags, and then we'll start snooping." Although all I want to do is curl up on the sofa and read a book.

There's three floors. The first floor is where the swimming pool, Jacuzzi, gym, and movie theater are, along with the kitchen, dining room, and what Lacey and I refer to as the ballroom although Mom said it's the entertaining room. The room is three times as big as our house in Phoenix. That's not an entertaining room, that's a ballroom, it's where the party will be tomorrow. The second floor houses the master bedroom and three other rooms, one of which Lacey is using, Harrison's office, and a spare bedroom. The third floor is where I am staying. There's only two bedrooms here, and a huge sitting room. Mom thinks Hudson and I could use it to get to know each other.

FOUR

Mia

"Mia, Lacey. Dinner's ready." Mom calls out, and I glance at Lacey, her pale skin is so noticeable in this light, as is the dark circles under her eyes. I wonder if my appearance is as haggard as hers? All I want to do is get in the shower and then collapse on the bed. Maybe even sleep for a week.

"Ugh food," Lacey groans and I can't help but laugh, "don't say it, Mia." She warns me.

I laugh harder, "I told you not to eat anything else." I smirk at her as she climbs out of the bed. "Coming, Mom," I yell. Harrison hasn't come home yet. I've been keeping a close eye on the window.

"Do you think your mom would mind having a housemate?"

I shake my head, "For the fifth time Lace, I don't think Harrison and Mom want you crashing their newly wedded bliss."

She pouts, "This house is amazing. I want to live in it forever."

This house is indeed amazing. There's a freaking swimming pool. I'll be making use of that while I'm here. Lacey found a wooded trail that she wants us to run tomorrow, we try and get out whenever we can, most of the time we don't. We're too lazy, but I have a feeling that tomorrow morning Lacey will be making me.

"What about college?" I ask and get flipped off in the process. She despises college, I'm the only reason she's able to make it through. "Lace, you're majoring in engineering, you're like a rocket scientist."

She rolls her eyes at me, "Engineering is nothing like rocket science. It's better. You really should go downstairs before your mom calls a search party to find you."

Placing the book down onto the sofa, I stand, "Um, not just me. Mom will be expecting the both of us."

She sways from side to side, "No, Mia, I'll stay in my room while you get to know your stepdad."

I groan, "No, that's not happening. You're here as a buffer." I tell her as I open the bedroom door, "Besides, you're a part of this family, you should get to know him too."

"I hate you." She grumbles, she's dreading this as much as I am, her for different reasons though. She thinks I'm going to make things awkward because I'm mad at them for how they've gone about things.

"You love me really. I keep you fed." I stick my tongue out at her as we begin walking down the stairs.

"Ah, there you two are, I was about to send out a search party," Mom says as we reach the bottom step. "Girls, Harrison's dying to meet you both."

"Mrs. Brady, I can't wait to meet him too," Lacey tells her with an easy smile.

"Lacey, how many times have I told you to call me Tina?" Mom tells her with a shake of her head. It doesn't matter how many times Mom says it, Lacey's always going to call her Mrs. Brady. "I hope you're both hungry, I went a bit overboard."

I laugh, "How much did you order in?"

She smiles as we walk into the dining room,

"Too much." Mom can't cook. She never has and never will; it's one of the many attributes I take from her.

"Nonsense Tina, we'll eat it all." A tall, handsome man tells her as he pulls her into his arms. He turns to me as he lets go of her, "You must be Mia." He holds his hand out for me to shake, I take it, grateful he's not pulling me in for a hug.

"Hi, it's nice to finally meet you," I tell him as I shake his hand. Looking up at him. I suck in a deep breath as I'm confronted by deep brown eyes that are so familiar to me, they remind me so much of my mystery man's. The man I had a one night stand with almost two years ago, the man I've constantly thought about since that night. Hell, I never even got his name, I'll never know who he is.

"Your mom has told me so much about you, the both of you." He looks to Lacey and shakes her hand too. "How's college going for you both?"

"How about we sit down and begin eating. I don't want the food getting cold. We can talk while we eat." Mom tells us and pulls me in for a hug.

"Lacey, how is your engineering course going?" Harrison asks, a warm smile on his face as we sit down, Mom really did go all out, there's plates filled with different foods. There's steak, chicken, and fish. There's also pasta, fries, potatoes, and a salad. Anything we could want, it's here, but there's way too much for the four of us.

I watch as Lacey's face lights up, he's treating her as though she's part of this family. I'm starting to really like him, he makes my mom happy, and he doesn't seem like an asshole. "I like it, it's hard, but it will be worth it when I graduate."

"What about you, Mia? How's your course going?" He doesn't sound as interested in mine as he did Lacey's, but it's what I'm used to, no one thinks majoring in English is anything spectacular.

"It's good. I love the creative aspect of it. Writing is a way of expressing ourselves, just as art is for others." I don't know why I feel so defensive about it.

His eyebrow raises in surprise, but that smile is still firmly on his face, it's not forced. "What do you plan on doing once you graduate?"

"I'm torn between becoming an English teacher or becoming an editor."

He looks impressed, "Your mom tells me that you love reading. What's your favorite book?"

I glance at Mom, her face turning pink while Lacey looks down at her plate and starts eating. "I like E.L. James, Carly Phillips, Harper Sloan, and Nora Roberts. I'd happily curl up with any one of their books."

He frowns, "I've heard of Nora Roberts, but haven't read any of her books, the others I can't say I've ever heard of them."

"Oh you'd have heard of E.L. James, she wrote Fifty Shades Of Grey." Lacey pipes up, and I watch in amusement as Harrison's face falls as he realizes exactly what Fifty is all about. "What about you, Mr. Brady, do you read?"

"I haven't read in a while. I like thrillers. Lee Child, James Patterson, Stephen King." He tells us as he reaches and takes a piece of steak.

"Have you read Harlan Coben? He writes some amazing thrillers like Drop Shot, One False Move, and Tell No One." I'm in my element now. This is safe ground, I love talking about books. I love almost every genre out there. I'll give anything a go once. Indie authors are my favorite as their work is so unique, it's like a diamond in the rough.

He shakes his head, "No, I must say I haven't."

Mom laughs, "He'll be buying those books now to read."

"You were right Tina, she *is* extremely passionate about books. The way her eyes light up when she recommended Harlan to me. She'll be fantastic as either a teacher or an editor."

I can feel myself begin to blush, "Thank you." I say and put my head down and start eating.

The dinner goes amazingly well, better than I had expected. The conversation flowed, and there was no awkwardness. I honestly came here thinking I'd hate Harrison, but it's quite the opposite. I like him, he and my mom seem really happy together. My dad's gone, and Harrison will never replace him. I know that now, so I'm just going to take it as it comes.

“Mrs. Brady, when is your party?” Lacey asks practically bouncing in her seat.

"Tomorrow evening, there will be at least two hundred guests here for the party," Mom says matter-of-factly as if that’s a normal thing to say.

I blink as Lacey gasps, "Two hundred?" I ask, making sure that I heard her correctly.

Harrison laughs, "Yes, two hundred. We never did celebrate our wedding properly and tomorrow night is a party to do just that."

Damn, that means that we have to attend.

"As I was saying..." Mom continues, "It's a formal party which means you both need new dresses."

Lacey and I look at each other and smile. New dresses, that's fine, we can make a day of it. "Cool, we'll go shopping in the morning."

"You can take Barney. He'll be your personal chauffeur for the day. Also, he has my credit card so you can buy whatever you want."

I instantly shake my head, "Thanks for the offer, but I thought Lacey and I could have a girls day and go shopping and relax before the party."

"Tina," Harrison says, there's a warning to his tone giving my mom a pointed look.

"Mia, listen to Harrison, okay? He's being nice and wants to treat you girls to a new dress." Mom tells us and gives Harrison a soft smile. I'm confused, I have no idea why she's so dead set on us spending his money, that's not who I am, and that's not how she raised me, but the pleading look in her eye makes me keep my mouth shut and nod.

"Excellent, Barney will be outside at nine-thirty ready to take you wherever you need to go." Harrison says as he throws his napkin onto the table and stands up, "Thank you for a wonderful dinner Tina, I'm just going to my office to make a couple of calls. I'll be down in a while." He kisses her cheek as he passes by her and walks out of the door.

"Want to tell me what that was about?" I ask Mom as soon as he's out of sight.

"Yeah, that was weird," Lacey comments, looking as suspicious as I feel.

Mom sighs, "Look, girls, Harrison is rich, extremely so. Barney is head of his security along with his driver. Harrison has a lot of enemies, and he doesn't want you girls caught up in the crossfire of someone trying to get at him. So please do as he says, he's only got your best interest at heart."

"Okay Mom," I say although I don't agree with it, I'll do it because I'm not wanting to argue with her or Harrison about it.

She smiles. "Good. Now, have you spoken to Sarah recently?"

I frown, "Yeah, I spoke to her yesterday, why?"

"Her mom's worried about her. She hasn't once been home since leaving for New York." Mom tells me, and I already know she hasn't, why would she when her life was shit when she lived here in Cali? "Dorothy was wondering if you had spoken to her and if you had that maybe you could talk to her about coming home?"

I sigh, "No, Mom, I won't. She has her reasons for not wanting to come home, and I completely understand those. I won't badger her to do it."

"I know she went through a lot while she was here. The bullying was horrendous, but Dorothy really misses her." Mom continues and Lacey shakes her head. She's met Sarah, it's something I've not told Mom, but Sarah comes and visits us sometimes and vice versa.

"Funny, she didn't seem to give a rat's ass about Sarah when her husband was beating on her." I say as I get to my feet, "I'm not asking her, Mom, and I can't believe you would even ask." I'm so pissed off right now, how dare she, she knows what Sarah went through trying to escape the hell that Oakland brought and yet she doesn't seem to give a crap.

"Mia, I asked, and you've said no. That's all there is to it. Don't get upset." Mom pleads with me.

I glance up at the clock on the wall. It's ten-thirty. I didn't realize how much time had passed since we came down for dinner at nine. "I'm going to bed. Lacey wants to go for a run in the morning before we go shopping. Goodnight," I tell her as I walk away. I'm taking myself away from this situation. I'm still mad and Mom's acting as if she did nothing wrong when in fact she knows she did.

"Mrs. Brady, thank you for a wonderful dinner, I'm going to turn in now too. Today has been a long day, and I find when traveling, I'm always tired just a little bit more than I usually would be. I'll see you in the morning." Lacey tells her diplomatically as she walks up beside me, her lips pursed into a thin line.

"Oh, of course. I should have known you'd both be tired. You've had a long day. Get some rest, so you're ready for the party tomorrow." Mom says taking the plates from the table and stacking them on top of one another.

"Goodnight Mom," I say as I exit the dining room.

"Are you going to call Sarah?" Lacey asks as we reach her bedroom.

"Yeah, she deserves to know that her mom's been trying to get her to come home. God, I hate that woman, she must be after something." Sarah is going to be pissed, and rightly so. Knowing Sarah though, she's going to call her mom and tell her to stop asking, she won't be coming home.

"Okay, I'm going to try and catch up on some of the course work that's due for when we get back."

I laugh, "You're such a nerd."

She pushes me away, "Says the woman who reads for fun. Night Mia."

"Night Lacey," I say and watch as she closes her bedroom door.

Walking past Harrison's office, I hear him talking. Well, more like growling. "What do you mean you won't be here for breakfast?" Everyone's mood seems to have dropped. "Hudson, your ass better be here for the party. Tina's excited to meet you. She's going to be upset now that you're no longer attending breakfast. She had hoped you'd meet Mia before the party."

I continue walking past his office and up the stairs, I need to call Sarah and then crawl into bed and read.

Reaching into my pocket, I take out my phone and dial Sarah's number. She answers right away. "Hey Mia, wishing you had stayed home?" She laughs, I've told her about Mom marrying Harrison and that I wasn't looking forward to meeting him. "What's he like?"

Walking into my bedroom, I close the door behind me. "He's actually really nice, not at all what I had imagined," I tell her as I climb onto the bed and lie down. "Mom asked about you today."

"Oh yeah? Is she missing me?" She laughs, "Oh shit, you're silent, what happened?"

She knows me too well. "Okay, so your mom's

been asking mine about whether or not we've been speaking and if we had could I get you to come home?" I'm still so angry about it.

"Christ! I've told her a million times before. I can't go home Mia. I'm finally happy with my life." Sadness creeps into her voice, and I know that she's not really happy, she wants more, but that's not going to happen yet so she's dealing with it the best way she can.

"I know, so how is Allie?" I ask her, "I miss her."

"She's good. She's finally starting to sleep through the night. I couldn't take much more of the lack of sleep. I was like a zombie." She does sound much better, maybe she *is* happy?

"I told you, Sarah, come to us anytime, Lacey and I love Allie, and we'll watch her while you catch up on sleep." I wish we lived closer. She's alone with a ten-month-old baby and no support system around her at all.

"I love you both. You don't know how much your support has meant to me."

Tears spring to my eyes, "Have you had any more thoughts about Jagger?"

When Sarah fell pregnant, she was scared. At first, she had no idea what to do. When she hit the six-month mark she decided she'd go to San Fran and see Jagger. He'd gotten back with Carina while she'd been gone, hell they could have reunited the next day for all we know. Sarah toyed with leaving them be and telling them, but ultimately she wanted her baby to know her dad and called Jagger. He didn't answer, but she got a voice message from Carina, they knew she was pregnant, how I don't know. The message left on her voice mail was horrible, and I hate Jagger for not having the balls to call Sarah himself. If he didn't want the baby that's fine, but to have Carina call and be a bitch wasn't necessary.

"I still haven't decided yet. I'm thinking I should contact him and let him know that I had Allie and if he ever changes his mind that she'd love to see him. I'm not a spiteful person Mia, I would never withhold Allie from him, he's her dad, and I would love if they got to have that bond that you had with yours. I was so envious, but it was so beautiful. That's what I want for my baby."

"I know you're not a spiteful person Sarah, the fact that you're willing to call him says everything. Maybe you should send him an email?"

She laughs, "An email? Mia, what century are you in?"

"Look, everyone needs an email address for

their phones. Besides, you can attach a picture of Allie. Because seriously, who could say no to her? She's such a happy smiley baby." Talking about her makes me miss her even more. I really need to take a trip to the big apple and see them both.

She sighs, "You're right. I'll do it tomorrow. I'll type out an email and attach a picture of Allie. God, what would I do without you?"

"You'll never have to find out. I'll call you tomorrow, okay?"

"Yeah, thanks Mia, for everything."

"Goodnight Sarah."

"Night Mia."

I end the call and just lie here, I'm physically drained. I feel bad for Sarah, she's been through so much, and yet she's a fighter. She's an amazing mom to Allie and a great friend. I'll arrange a trip with Lacey for us this summer, it'll be good to see them both.

As soon as I close my eyes, I'm haunted by those deep brown eyes of my mystery guy. Every night he invades my dreams. Our night together replays over and over in my mind. My hand goes into my panties, and I let the images of us together play out as I begin to play with myself.

FIVE

Hudson

The sound of my cell ringing has me looking at Jagger, "It's my dad, tell everyone the meeting is in an hour, anyone not in attendance better be dying or else they're going to wish they were." I say through clenched teeth.

"Will do Boss." He tells me with a smile. The man is a fucking sadistic sonofabitch. He comes across as a sweet southern boy, but in actual fact, he's a stone-cold killer. He's my right-hand man, everything he does is on my say so.

"Hey, old man, everything good?" I ask as I answer the phone, noticing Jagger's smirk as he leaves my office, he'll have the boys rounded up and ready for a meeting. If anyone disobeys, he'll deal with them.

"Less of the old, thank you. I'm just calling to see what time you'll be here in the morning?"

I close my eyes and silently curse. Shit, I forgot about that fucking breakfast. "Sorry Dad, there's been a change of plans. I won't be there for breakfast."

"What do you mean you won't be here for breakfast?" He growls. The old man's pissed.

"Dad, I'm sorry, but I've got business to take care of."

"Hudson, your ass better be here for the party. Tina's excited to meet you. She's going to be upset now that you're no longer attending breakfast. She had hoped you'd meet Mia before the party." His voice vibrating with anger.

"Dad, I'll be there. You left me with a fucking shit storm that I'm trying to sort out. So it takes precedence over a breakfast. I'll be there for that party."

My dad used to run my business until he met Tina, he fell in love, and she told him that she wouldn't be with someone who lived the life he did. So he did the only thing he could do to keep the woman he loves. He gave up the title of boss and handed it to me. I was grateful, it was something I had been working toward. I always knew that when my father stepped down, I would take over, but no one expected it to happen this quickly. At twenty-seven, many believe I'm too young, that I'm too much of a hothead to lead this organization, and yet, here I am. I'm cleaning up the shit my father left us in. He went into business with the cartel, something I had strongly suggested against but he didn't listen, and now I'm stuck with a fucking piece of shit as my business partner.

"Watch it son." He warns me, "I may no longer be in charge, but you had better show some damn respect."

I laugh, "I do, I've shown you respect my entire life and yet when I told you not to do business with Juan, you chose to ignore me, and now I'm having to deal with his shit."

He sighs, "I know, okay, but think of the long run. Juan has connections down south that we don't have nor could we ever get."

He always thought of this business like a game of chess. Always at least one step ahead, most of the time he was four or five steps ahead, he planned everything out to a T and yet, he didn't plan for Tina to happen. Falling for her fucked everything up, she consumed him, and this organization suffered. Yet he jumped into business with Juan

Álverez, of the Álverez Cartel without listening to the protests and now I'm stuck with the fucker.

"I still don't trust the guy. He's a liability. Not only that, my own men don't think I'm capable for this job. They're waiting on me to fuck up."

He laughs, "Then don't."

My office door opens, and Jagger walks in, his jaw tight. Great, something has happened. "Dad, I've got to go. I'll be at the party." I assure him.

"Okay son..." The line goes silent, and I know he wants to say something, "I'll see you tomorrow." Whatever he wants to say he can't. He no longer has a say in what goes on inside this operation. I'm not opposed to going to him if I need advice, I just won't tolerate him back seat driving.

"Bye." I hang up and give Jagger my full attention, "What?"

He sighs, "We've got a problem."

I give him a hard stare. I gathered that we had a problem.

"Carina, she's fucked up." He admits, and it's about fucking time, he's been keeping everything with that bitch close to his chest.

"I know she's a fuck-up, what's she done now?" I hate that woman. I'd love nothing more than to wrap my hands around her throat and choke the life out of her. I've been close on many occasions but because she's Jagger's girl I won't.

"Got a phone call from Jax, she's high as a fucking kite." He's pacing my office, his jaw clenched so tightly it's a wonder he's not breaking his damn teeth.

Great, the bitch has been sampling our merchandise, let’s hope she fucking paid for it herself.

"What are you going to do Jag? That woman is a fucking mess." I shake my head in disgust; everything she does is vile.

"I'm done with her. I can't fucking do this." Anger dripping from his words.

"You should have been done with her a long ass time ago. If you had you'd have made sure you tied that blonde to the bed." I give him a pointed look. I have no idea who the woman is; all I know is two women walked into our lives on the same night and fucked with our heads. Both women vanished before sunrise, never to be seen or heard from again.

He narrows his eyes at me, "You think I don't think about that constantly? Sarah was fucking amazing, and now she’s disappeared."

"You ever think having that bitch on your dick

could have been the reason why?" I have my suspicions about Carina and the shit she's said to keep Jagger on a hook. She was here the night Jagger and Sarah got together, and I'm betting my left nut she's lying about everything.

His eyes flash with anger, "I'm not fucking stupid Hudson, I know what she's been doing."

I give him a look, one that tells him to watch his tone. "Then what the fuck were you still doing with her?"

He sighs, "Leave it, yeah? We've got a meeting to get to."

"Jag, I get you're pissed. That bitch has you wrapped around her finger. You became her lap dog…"

His eyes narrow, "Boss…"

I raise an eyebrow, "Jag, you've lost the respect from some of the men, as my right-hand man that can't be allowed. It's going to take you a fucking long time to rebuild that respect. Carina was yours to control, and you failed to do so. That's on you." I tell him, he's my brother, but he's fucked up. Women do not feature in our world; they're to be cherished and protected. They do not treat the men as their personal slaves or as someone beneath them.

"Everyone going to be there?" I ask as I exit my office.

"Yes." He replies, walking beside me. "I almost laughed when I got a reply from Ulric telling me he'll be there."

I smirk. This is going to be fun. "He's not going to know what's hit him."

As we get outside the club, there's a black sedan across the street. Fucking feds, always up in my business. They're trying to find anything on me to put me inside. I'm not that fucking stupid.

"Mr. Brady," Johnson calls out, that guy is really busting his chops to try and pin something on me, he's a rookie fed, and he's hoping that if he can get me in the can, it'll make his career. He'll be a legend, bringing down the biggest drug lord in America.

"Mr. Johnson, don't you have anything better to do? Like going home to your family?" I smirk, the fucker is a loner, his wife left him because he was fucking his co-worker. So he spends his evenings trying to find anything to bring my organization down.

His lips thin into a tight line. "You going anywhere nice?"

I give him a cold stare, "That would be none of

your business. I'll see you around, Mr. Johnson." I climb into the back of the Bentley Continental, Jagger climbing in beside me as Martin starts the engine.

"He's got a hard on for you Hudson. He's not going to let up." Jagger grinds his teeth. He does that when he's mad, it's his tell. The one that tells you to run because Jagger's on the warpath.

"Tell me about it. He needs to look elsewhere and fast. I can't have him on my ass." The fucker is way too close for my liking.

"Martin, did you service the car?" That's Jagger's way of asking if Martin swept for bugs and tracking devices.

"It's fine," he's a man of very limited words. Just how I like it. I hate small talk, it's useless and pointless.

The car's clean, there's no way Martin would lie. Besides Jagger, he's the most loyal man I have. He's killed men for betraying me. He started out as my driver when he first started working for the family and grew into my bodyguard. I never needed him, I'm more than capable of fighting my own battles, but Dad was boss and what he said went. So a twenty-two year old Martin became my chauffeur and bodyguard when I was fifteen.

"Martin, what's happening with Jorge? Has he given you any information?" I ask, feeling irritated, I hate being kept in the dark.

It's been two weeks and no contact from him. He's been in the Álverez Cartel for over a year, long before we joined forces with Juan, but when my dad left and he found out about my dislike of Juan, he came forward. He told us that he'd feed us information in return for making sure his wife and child who live here in San Francisco are safe while he can't be with them. He doesn't trust Juan, and he had suspicions that his family were being watched. He was right; they were. I managed to get them into a safe house and no one, not even Jagger knows where they are. Jorge was true to his word, and he has fed us vital information. I haven't made any of what he's said public yet. I'm biding my time. Getting all my ducks in a row, if things go south, I'm making sure there's no blowback on us. Jorge hasn't given anything to us in the last two weeks, and I'm getting fucking antsy.

"Yes Boss. He's given me something, and I'm not sure of its authenticity, so I'm doing some checks before I inform you." He says cryptically, and I raise my brow, does he really believe that shitty response is going to keep me from inquiring further?

I glance at Jagger, who looks just as shocked as I do. "Martin?" I growl, he's pissed me off with the bullshit he's just said.

A heavy sigh escapes him, "Boss, he heard something that didn't sit right with him, he confided that to me, and we're not sure if it's credible."

"Credible?" My entire body vibrating with anger.

Jagger lets out a chuckle, "Marty boy, you'd want to talk."

"Fuck. You're a hot-headed sonofabitch." Martin murmurs, "Jorge overheard a conversation where Juan was discussing your new family."

My eyes narrow, "What about my new family?"

Martin's shoulders lift as he shrugs, "Jorge didn't hear the entire conversation. He thinks it's a threat, but we've yet to verify if it is or not."

I grit my teeth, I know he expects me to fly off the handle. He's right, I'm a hothead, and I do things on the fly. Being the boss means I can't do that anymore. I need to think with a clear head.

"Is Juan in town? Or anyone associated with him? Did Jorge say who he was talking to? Or who may be the one to carry out the threat if it was, in fact, a threat?" I throw out question after question, and there's a surprised but pleased look on Martin's face. Jagger looks shocked. I ignore them and wait for the answers to my questions.

"Juan is in town," Jagger informs me looking at his cell phone. His eyes narrow as he reads whatever is on his phone.

"How do you know that he's in town?" The more important question is, *why* is he here?

Jagger shrugs, "I saw him earlier near the club. I assumed he'd been in to see you."

"What have I said about making assumptions?" Fuck, I need to have the footage of the club checked to make sure he wasn't snooping. Fucker, there was no reason as to why he should be near my club.

He doesn't answer, instead his jaw tenses. He's pissed. Whether it's at me or himself, I couldn't give a shit. He's my right-hand man, that means he should know if that asshole was scheduled for a meeting today.

"I've been checking on his associates and have yet to find one that's here. Jorge says that he doesn't know the man Juan was talking to, that he has only been seen once or twice in the compound. Boss, I told you what he told me, that's all I know, and that's why I wanted to check it out. I have no idea if the information relayed to me is a threat or just a mindless discussion."

And here I was thinking the man had brains. "There's no need to be discussing my family. Ever." He made a fucking mistake, one that is going to be deadly for him.

Jagger lets out a low whistle, "This meeting is going to be fun." He smirks as he rubs his hands together.

I shake my head. He's a bloodthirsty fucker. He smiles when things go south. He's the only man I know that loves to be against the ropes, he comes out swinging and always wins.

"I'm taking bets that Ulric's going to do one of three things..." Martin begins.

Jagger's brows raise as he interrupts him. "Dude, only one, you can't take three. I'm going to say he cries. He'll weep and call for his mom."

"Ass." Martin mutters, "I've twenty on him pissing himself."

"You're on!" Jagger hoots.

I chuckle, these two saps have nothing better to do than bet on what Ulric's going to do when I walk in and point my gun at his kneecap. You don't fucking betray me. Ever.

"Looks like we've got a full house Boss," Martin informs me as he drives up to the abandoned lot, it's far enough away from the city lights to give us privacy and yet not too far away that it takes a fucking age to get to.

Getting out of the car, I gaze at the abandoned lot and curse. I'm going to have to find a new place to hold my meetings, somewhere the feds don't know about. Walking into the lot, the chatter that filled the room is now a deathly silence, every man's eyes are on me as I walk in. I have thirty-three men, and I glance around the room at them. The newest members are at the back, they've probably heard rumors of what's about to happen. They're about to get a rude awakening. The men that have been with me since the get-go, the ones that called me Boss before I had the title are lean, well kept, and smartly dressed. Whereas the men that have been here since my dad and gramps were boss are overweight, balding and insubordinate.

Fucking Ulric has a smirk on his face as he stands with his arms crossed. That look he has further adds fuel to my anger. I purposely stride toward him and everyone between us parts like it's the Red Sea. Only Cage and Darwin stand beside him; they had better move when the shit hits the fan. I'll take them both out too. I have no problem emptying house if need be as long as my men fall in line.

My hand automatically goes to my gun located at my back, my fingers tighten around the butt. "Ulric." My voice cold and I watch as that smirk falls from his face. "Did you really think I wouldn't find out?"

Cage and Darwin take a step away from him. Good, they're making it clear they don't align with him.

"Fin…" He licks his lips as he stands a little taller, his eyes flashing with fear as the gun comes out from behind my back. "Find out what?" He manages to stammer out.

"That you betrayed me." My voice is calm. It's funny, when I'm angry I can go one of two ways: lose my head and go gonzo on everyone around me, or I can be a methodically calm sonofabitch. That's what I'm doing right now.

His eyes widen, "No, I didn't."

I glance around the room. Every single person's eyes are on me, waiting to find out what I'm going to do. "Lying to me as well as betraying me. You really are a fucking idiot."

I hear snickering from behind me, and I know that it's Jagger and Martin.

His hands raise, "I didn't, I swear to you Hudson, I didn't betray you. I wouldn't."

I aim my gun at his knee, "Oh, so the footage I have of you talking with Detective Collins is fake? You had a great discussion with the man Ulric. You talked with him for *thirty-three minutes*." My finger squeezes the trigger, and I watch with a smile as the bullet rips into his leg, he instantly buckles and falls to the floor. I walk over to him, my gun still raised at his face.

"No." He cries out, tears streaming down his face. Fucking weasel. "Please Hudson, please just let me explain." He begs.

"It's Mr. Brady to you." I tell him with disdain, “You betrayed me, and you’ve betrayed my men, your brothers. Snitching to a fucking cop is going to make us all go down you pathetic moron.”

“Please….” He stammers as tears begin to fall down his face.

“No, no, please nothing. You fucked up, and you pay the consequences.” My tone is even. He’s fucked up and big time. This is something I cannot forgive, and I won’t forgive.

The room is quiet; the only thing you can hear is Ulric's crying.

"Martin pay up, Jag was right, he's crying like a damn baby." I stare hard at the sobbing mess that's beneath my feet, "Listen up, and listen good." I say, my voice strong and loud, making sure every man in here hears me. "I don't give a shit if you think that I shouldn't be here. I earned my place here. It was always going to be me that was going to take over. Don't like the fact I'm younger than most of you? That's your problem, you either get over it, or you're going to end up like Ulric here." He's squirming, the tears falling down his face but he's no longer begging me, he knows that he fucked up and there's no way he's getting out of here alive. My finger squeezes the trigger once again. This time the bullet goes into his head.

Turning around, I face my men. Each one of them has a blank expression. "Show me respect and loyalty, and I'll give it back tenfold. Betray me, and it'll be the last thing you do. Most of you have been with this organization for decades. You saw what a hot-headed little shit I was and when I gave no thought to anyone but myself. It's time for you to realize that I'm no longer a child and that I'm your boss now. Don't like it? There's a bullet here for you."

A few uneasy shuffles from the older guys, the guys that thought my dad wouldn't pass the job to me until he was in his sixties, hell most thought Dad would be buried before he'd give up the crown.

"You're pissed because my old man left, be pissed at him. I want my men behind me. I want to know that they trust me and that I can trust them." This is the only time I'm going to have this speech; anyone who doesn't fall in line is gone. I don't have the time nor the patience for this crap anymore. It's ending tonight. I made Ulric an example. They needed to know what is going to happen when you betray me, betray the family.

"Anyone have a problem with that?" I stare each and every one of them down, waiting to see if any of them will have the balls to go against me. Some are glancing at their shoes, others are focusing their gazes beyond me. My boys, the ones that have been calling me Boss for years are nodding in agreement. I turn to face Carmine. He's one of the men that's glancing at their shoes.

"Good, get rid of him and this gun." I glare at Matt and Carmine Jr. They were both my father's soldiers. They thought they'd move up the ranks, but they never did. It's because they're lazy and that shit isn't going to fly anymore.

"Cage, find out where Detective Collins is, and see if you can find out what the traitor told him. Then get rid of him." I instruct, he gives me a sharp nod and leaves.

"Burn this place to the ground," Jagger tells Matt and Carmine as I begin to walk out of the lot. "Not with him inside." He adds, knowing just how fucking lazy they can be.

At least this shit is done now. It's time to focus on making sure that Juan doesn't try and fuck me over. He's already on borrowed time. He comes after my family, he's going to suffer.

SIX

Mia

"God, we really need to work out more, we're both so unfit." My breath comes in pants as I place my hand against the wall and try and suck in some much-needed oxygen. I actually can't remember when I ran so hard. It was refreshing, but I'm going to pay for it later.

I am, however, faring a bit better than Lacey is. She's sprawled on the floor, her face bright red, and her entire body is shaking. "I'm dying." She whispers and I laugh, such dramatics.

I was awoken at seven this morning by a smiley Lacey who demanded we go for a run. Looking at her now, I'd say she's regretting it, and it's going to be a while before she's wanting to do it again. Once I'm able to get my breathing under control, I reach down and help Lacey up. "Come on, we need to have a shower. I can hear movement in the kitchen, here's hoping that Harrison's good at cooking because I'm starved."

"That man is a lot of things, but I doubt he's a cook. I did a bit of digging after dinner." She begins, and I just know where this is going to go.

I shake my head. "This isn't the place. We'll talk about this later." I wouldn't be surprised if Mom was listening. That woman has ears like a bat, and she's always around somewhere.

"Okay. Did you speak to Sarah?" She asks as we walk towards the door.

"Yeah, we spoke about her contacting Jagger." I spit his name out. I despise that man. "The private investigator she used got her an email address for him. She's going to send him an email and attach a picture of Allie. It's about time he manned up. He may not have wanted Allie, but he needs to know that she's alive. He helped create an amazing child. For Allie's sake I hope he reads the email and contacts Sarah. Allie needs her dad in her life."

Lacey links her arm through mine, "She really does, can you imagine her little face lighting up when she sees him? How is Sarah?"

"Lonely and busy, I was thinking of arranging

for us to see them sometime this summer, maybe toward the end?" She's not really made any friends since being in New York. Having a baby alone in a new city with no support was the hardest thing anyone could have done, and I admire her so much for doing it. She's thriving as a mom and as a designer, she's finally starting to have her designs noticed by Leila Del La Core. She's the best designer in the world, and she noticed Sarah's designs on Instagram of all places. Since then they've been working together to get a fall range designed. It's being showcased in September for Fashion Week, so she's busy.

Lacey's eyes light up. "New York during summer break? Why are you even asking?"

I laugh, I knew she'd want to go. When I left Oakland, Sarah and I were great friends. Now we're best friends, sisters even and now we've found one more, Lacey. We're all as thick as thieves even though Sarah lives over two thousand miles away.

"Do you think Sarah will bring us to Fashion Week?" Lacey asks as we walk up the stairs.

"Fashion Week?" Mom's voice asks from behind us, and I inwardly groan, I knew she was around somewhere, I wonder how long she was listening for.

"Yeah Mom, Sarah's working with a designer and her designs will be showcased during Fashion Week." I inform her, "Can we talk about this at breakfast? I want to have a shower."

Her lips press into a thin line as hurt flashes in her eyes, "Of course, is there anything you'd like for breakfast?"

I give her a smile, "Everything!" We all laugh, but I'm serious. "Mom, I could eat everything and anything. I'm starving. Lacey made me go for a run. I swear I must have ran at least half a marathon."

Lacey rolls her eyes, "Hardly, we ran six miles, Mia. That's nowhere near half a marathon. But I'm hungry too."

Mom laughs, "I'll get the maid to make you both a full breakfast."

I grin, "The maid?"

Mom's eyes roll, "Yes, she's a housemaid who also cooks because both Harrison and I are completely useless. She's here today as she's cleaning the house."

"Cool, what's her name?" I ask, "Has she always worked for Harrison?"

"Her name is Willa, and she's only been working with us for a week. Harrison wanted a housemaid, so I interviewed a few ladies and Willa was the best. Anyway, you two go ahead and get showered. Breakfast will be ready when you come down." Mom says before glancing to her left. "Go," she claps her hands and both Lacey and I laugh and run up the stairs.

"We've less than an hour before Barney is here. We'd better hurry, I'd hate to keep the poor man waiting." Lacey says, and I'm shocked that she remembered his name, I forgot. "Don't wash your hair. We'll do it tonight as we get ready for the party."

"Sounds good, won't take me much more than fifteen minutes to be ready." I tell her as I walk toward the stairs, "If you're ready before me, make your way downstairs and have breakfast." Even as I say the words I know that I'll be ready before Lacey, she takes ages in the shower.

"Like that will ever happen. But same applies to you, we all know how much you like your food."

I laugh, "Okay, because I'm the person who went to an all you can eat buffet and went back six times." I roll my eyes as she snorts. "You're the greediest person I know Lace. I have no idea where you put it all."

She doesn't answer me; instead, she does the really mature thing by sticking her tongue out at me. I laugh at her as I run up the stairs toward my bedroom, there's no ensuite bathroom in my room whereas there is in Lacey's. Thankfully Hudson isn't here, so I have free rein over the bathroom which makes things easier.

"So you did some digging?" I ask Lacey as we sit down to get some lunch, we've been shopping for hours and we've bought everything except for dresses for this evening. Barney has been dutifully following us around, he's six foot five and built like a linebacker. With the name Barney, I had thought he'd be some scrawny guy, but he's not. He's also a lot younger than I had thought. I'm guessing he's in his mid-to-late- twenties, if not his early thirties. Lacey's eyes immediately lit up when she saw him.

"Right, so after everything that Greg had said and the lavish lifestyle he leads, I guess I just wanted to know who he was." Her voice's low as an anxiousness mars her face.

"Why are you fretting?" I reach over and grab her shaky hand. I wonder what she's found out, she seems to be frightened, but of what?

She worries her lip between her teeth as she glances around the diner we're in. "Mia." She whispers, "I didn't find anything. I mean nothing at all. There's no trace, not that I could find."

My eyes widen, holy shit! If Lace can't find anything that's huge. Lacey is a whiz with a computer, she can find out anything about anyone.

"I called Greg this morning before we left. I wanted to find out what he knew." She glances around the room again, almost as if she's expecting someone to be watching us.

My nerves are skyrocketing. "Christ Lace, what did he say?"

"He told me that Hudson is the boss, he's a drug dealer Mia, he's a pimp and gun runner. It's a family business. His father was in charge before Hudson and his grandfather before that. His grandfather started it up, or his great grandfather, he wasn't sure. Mia, these people are dangerous." She implores with me just as Barney walks towards us, "Mia, Greg says they've killed people." Her voice is shaky as tears shine in her eyes

I glance at Barney and then back to Lacey, "I'll talk to Mom, she's not going to lie to me about something like this. I'll find out the truth." I promise her, she's frightened, and she's going to be even worse when we get back to the house.

"Ladies," Barney says coming to stand beside our table.

Lacey blushes, well at least she's not terrified anymore.

"Barney, why don't you join us for lunch? We've not long ordered." I tell him and watch as Lacey instantly nods, oh she's got it bad.

He glances around the diner, "I shouldn't."

Lacey rolls her eyes, "No one's here to tell you otherwise, besides, you must be hungry and this is on us. Our way of saying thanks for being a good sport for not once complaining while we've been shopping."

He doesn't say anything, but I can see him wavering.

"Or, think of it as a bribe for later on, we've still got to find dresses," I tell him and watch as he shakes his head. "It's up to you. Personally, I think you need to refuel. Shopping with us is a workout."

He laughs, "Fine. You've twisted my arm. I'll find the waitress and give her my order." He looks at Lacey, "If you think shopping is a workout, you've seriously been doing it wrong. I can show you if you'd like." I watch as his eyes darken,

Lacey's mouth parts in surprise before she slowly smirks. The look they're giving each other can only be described as sexual.

They stare at each other for what feels like an age. "I feel like I need to take a shower after watching you two."

Barney smiles before walking over to where the waitress is. "Holy shit." I gasp as soon as he's out of earshot. "Lacey, you two have some serious chemistry."

Her smile is one of the brightest I have seen from her. "I don't even know him, and I have this pull toward him."

I click my fingers, "I had that with my mystery guy. I swear it was like a magnet pulling me toward him. I just knew that going home with him that night was the right thing to do. Would you...?" I trail off as I know she's understands what I'm trying to say without having to actually say it.

She shrugs, "I don't know Mia, how do you even approach a subject like that when you've hardly spoken?"

I hold my hands up, "You're asking the wrong person. I've had sex with one person Lace, and you know how that went. He initiated it. It was amazing. But I have no idea where to even begin. It's like murky waters for me."

"Ah now, it's not that hard. You like someone, fuck 'em."

I turn and see Barney standing beside the table. "Jesus!" I cry out, "Where the hell did you come from?"

"How long have you been standing there?" Lacey asks him with narrowed eyes. "You should come with a bell."

He smirks as he slides into the seat beside Lacey, "You two were talking, I didn't want to interrupt."

I scoff, "What was that then?"

He winks at me, "Helping a sister out."

I shake my head. I'm not mad at him, he's like an annoying brother that I never had. His smile is infectious. He's a fun guy, one that I actually like.

"Soooo," Lacey asks, not looking at him. "Exactly how much did you hear?"

"Enough to know Mia needs to get laid."

I groan. "Seriously?"

Both he and Lacey smile, "Mia, when was the last time you had sex, or should I say the only time you had it?" Barney questions me.

I gape at him in disgust, "That would be none of your business."

"Nearly two years ago now," Lacey tells him for me. "She doesn't even know his name."

"Lace!" I choke, will she shut up?

"What? He heard everything anyway."

Barney nods, "I did, look, Mia, this guy sounds like an ass. Why haven't you moved on?"

"Wow Barney, are you getting serious with me?" I'm impressed; there's more to him than I first thought.

He tilts his head to the side and stares at me, "Mia, there's a reason you've not found someone else isn't there?" He says, and I'm starting to hate him.

"I have no idea what you're talking about. I've just been busy with school and everything." I glare at Lacey in hopes that she'll save me from this line of questioning.

His face tells me that he thinks I'm full of crap, but I ignore it and hope that the waitress comes down with our food and soon.

"What about you Lacey, do you have a mystery guy?" He asks her, his voice deep and soothing, he's very forward with his questioning.

"Nope, don't have time." She flashes him a quick smile. "What about you, Barney?" Her voice husky. "Do you have a lady, mysterious or otherwise?" She asks looking up through her lashes. She's good, she managed to come back with her own invasive questions.

I just shake my head at these two. I feel as though I'm intruding. Like I'm a third wheel. Every look they give each other is scorching hot.

"There's no specific lady in my life if that's what you're asking." Wow, he's a jerk, there was no need to answer it like that.

Lacey's eyes flash with disappointment, he's blown it with her. "I wonder how much longer our lunch is going to be." She's trying to put on a brave face, I can hear the strain in her voice.

"Hungry again?" I ask her teasingly, and I watch as her body relaxes a bit. "We should have gone to Taco Bell or McDonalds, somewhere quick."

She sighs, "Hell, they've not even brought our drinks down to us yet."

I glance at Barney, he's checking his phone, but his jaw is clenched, the muscles in his face tight. He knows he fucked up. It's his own damn fault. He really should think before he speaks.

My phone vibrates against the table, and I pick it up to see it's a text message from Sarah. "She sent the email." I inform Lacey, "God, I hope he responds."

She slumps back against the booth, "Now it's a waiting game. God, I'm so nervous for her."

"For who?" Barney chimes in.

"Our friend," I reply not really paying attention as I type out a message to send back to her.

"What happened?" He's genuinely curious.

I glance at Lacey. It's up to her if she wants to tell him. I would, but he's hurt Lace with a few stupid words.

"She had a one night stand with a guy she liked, he was in an off and on relationship." She shakes her head, "Long story short, she got pregnant and she called him. He had his girlfriend call her back and tell her that he didn't want the baby and he didn't want her." Her words clipped, she's still mad that Jagger did that too Sarah.

"She wanted him to know that he has a daughter, that if and when he wants to know Allie, that he can call and she'll set it up. That was the email she sent today." I finish, and it hurts to hear what Sarah went through, knowing that he could reject them yet again makes me want to cry.

"Wow, sounds like your friend is well shot of him. Anyone who gets their girlfriend to end things is an asshole. He made that baby, he should man up and take responsibility." He glances at both mine and Lacey's shocked faces, "What?"

I shrug, "I guess, we never really got a man's perspective on it before. We hate Jagger, what he did, fuck he's an asshole. I really hope I don't meet him while I'm here. I won't be held responsible for what I may do."

He nods, "That he is, where's your girl now?"

"New York, she's working in fashion," Lacey says proudly.

He frowns, "Are you from San Fran?" He asks, looking at me with a weird expression.

I shake my head, "No, I'm from Oakland, as is Sarah."

His eyes flash with something that resembles anger, "You said the man's name is Jagger? Where did your friend meet him?"

Now I'm confused. "Synergy."

He nods, "Great club."

My cheeks flame as I think back to the only night I was in it, fuck, it was a great night. "Yeah, it is." Movement in my peripheral vision has me glancing at the approaching waitress. "Finally," I mumble, we've still got to find dresses yet.

We walk into Mona Lora's Boutique, I glance

back at Barney, while we were eating he was really quiet and furiously texting on his phone. Now he's on his cell talking in a hushed tone. When he catches me watching him, he glares at me and turns around. I shake my head and continue into the store. Twenty minutes later and both Lacey and I have found our dresses.

"You'll be cleared of duty soon," Lacey tells him.

"Yep." He clips, anger pulsating from him.

"Whatever," I say and pull Lacey with me as we pay for them. Whatever his problem is, is just that - his. He doesn't need to be an ass to Lacey and I.

Walking around the ballroom, I'm surprised by how many people are actually here. There's way more than the two hundred guests here. If I were to guess, I'd say there's at least double that. Each and every one of them are clinging onto every word Mom and Harrison say. A waitress walks around with a tray of champagne in her hands, and I can't help myself, my arm reaches for a glass, and I bring it to my mouth. This party is boring as hell.

"Where did you get that from?" Lacey asks coming to stand beside me, where I was hiding in the corner, hoping and praying that no one comes up to me and congratulates me on having such a wonderful stepfather. "I want one." She pouts as she searches the room.

I point to the woman walking around with a tray in her hand. "The waitress is handing them out, be quick about it though. If Mom sees us with them, she'll have a heart attack."

She nods quickly before making her way over to the waitress. My eyes find Mom. She's in the middle of a conversation with some women. They remind me of Stepford wives. They're standing with their back straight, their movements robotic as they sip their drinks or laugh. This party isn't about a celebration, it's about flaunting their wealth, and I'm dying to escape. Looking back to Lacey, she's talking to Barney, a drink in hand, her eyes narrowed. Barney sure knows how to piss her off.

"Ugh." Lacey groans as she comes to stand beside me once again. "He's a jerk, there's something seriously wrong with him."

"What now?" I ask, finding this highly amusing even though she calls him a jerk, she wants him.

"He apologized, and I accepted it, but his cell

rang and just like that," She clicks her fingers, "he's back to being an ass. He's giving me whiplash."

A hush of silence falls over the room, and I glance up to see what's got everyone so quiet. My eyes meet the deepest brown set of eyes that I have ever seen, ones that haunt my dreams. My breathing stops as I stare at the man that I've not been able to get off of my mind.

"Mia?" Lacey questions, "Are you okay?"

"It's him," I whisper, my hand reaching out to grab a hold of hers. "It's my mystery man." I peer at her, and her eyes are on him too.

Her mouth pops open, "But Mia, that's Hudson."

I gasp, as butterflies swarm in my stomach. What the hell is he doing here? “Fuckity fuck,” I mutter as he walks towards us. That’s the man that I slept with. My mystery man, the one that I’ve had deep dark fantasies about, is my stepbrother.

SEVEN

Hudson

"Son, tell me you didn't," Dad says as I sit beside him on the bench.

When he called and asked me to meet him here at Golden Gate Park, I knew that he was going to start his shit.

"Didn't what?" There's no mistaking my tone. I don't like being questioned, especially from my own father.

"The fire, the body. It was a fucking cop. Christ." He shakes his head as his fist clenches, "Tell me something Hudson, was I wrong to hand the reins over to you?"

"Fuck no." I fire back, "What happened last night, it was my way of regaining control of the men that had begun to wane. The men that had put their trust in you, the men that believed they'd retire when they were too old, just as you would. The men that don't believe that I'm capable of the job. Don't sit there and make assumptions. You know nothing. Nothing. I was in shit creek because of your rash actions, and now I'm finally fixing it."

He intakes a sharp breath, followed by another, and another. He's calming himself down, not wanting to say something he'll regret. People wonder where I get being a hothead from? My dad. "Son, I know that things with Tina went a lot faster than any of us had imagined, but she's the only woman that I've loved."

I bite my tongue; he treated my mom like shit for years, always cheating on her. Making her out to be the reason as to why he was stepping out on her, that she was the reason he was acting the way he did. I hate him for the way he treated her but he's my dad, he was my boss, there was nothing I could do about it. The shit he says about how he and Tina are in love pisses me off, if she's the only woman he loved, then why the hell was he stringing Mom along for so damn long?

"Tina gave me an ultimatum. It was her or the organization."

I let out a bitter laugh, "Nice, Dad, you chose her over your family." I spit the word out, and he doesn't react. "Is there a particular reason you wanted to meet? Because it sure as hell wasn't to talk about what may or may not have happened last night."

"Will you be at the party tonight?"

Of course, he's checking to make sure that I'm going to be there to see my new stepmom and step-sister, God, I can't think of anything worse. "I've said I'll be there, so I'll be there." I stand, "Are we done?" I need to meet the men and get a status update of what went down last night after I left them.

He sighs as he stands, "Yeah, we're done."

I shake my head. He doesn't get what a mess he handed me when he passed on the crown. It was a poison chalice, one that I'm still trying to find an antidote for. "I'll see you tonight," I say and begin to stride towards my Bentley. He doesn't say anything and I carry on walking, not surprised that he's silent. He chose to leave this world, he needs to remember that. Climbing into the back of the car, I just settle into the seat when my cell begins to ring. Seeing Jagger's name on the screen makes me wonder what the hell Carina's done this time. Every time he calls me the bitch has fucked up in one way or another.

"What's she done now?" It's my way of a greeting. Martin begins to drive, his hands tight against the wheel. Seems it's a day for everyone to be in a pissy mood.

"Boss," His voice vibrates with anger.

"Have you killed anyone?"

He chuckles, "No, not yet although I'm fucking close."

"Right, is it any of the men?" I can't have him in a room with them if it is.

"No."

"Meet me and the rest of the men. We're having a meeting then you and I will have one." It's an order. He can't go off and kill who he pleases, although I'm pretty sure it's Carina that he's trying not to put his hands on. We may be assholes, but we don't stoop that low. Any of my men are found to have hit a woman, they will be severely dealt with, things are going to be different than how my dad ran the organization.

Martin's uncharacteristically silent, "What?" I bark out, the silence putting me on edge.

"I got a call from Jorge." I'm all ears. "The man that met with Juan is Juan's cousin, Arturo."

"How the hell did he not know it was his damn cousin?"

"Arturo's been in Mexico Boss. He's only been in the States for a month." Martin has a smirk on his face which means he has an idea. I wait for him to spit it out. "Arturo's visa ran out two weeks ago. It's time to have his ass deported."

I shake my head at the pettiness but fuck, it's a good idea. "Get the ball rolling, make sure he's arrested first and foremost with possession." Getting him arrested will have the cops look into him, he'll be deported for being an illegal. The cops on my payroll will see to it. Not only that, it'll add more heat onto Juan and give me even more excuse to keep that fucker away from my family and business.

"On it Boss, he'll be picked up by the end of the day." He assures me, and I smile. It's about time those fucking cops and officials on my payroll are being used. Otherwise, they're sitting on their asses doing fucking nothing while reaping the rewards.

"Boss, may I speak freely?" He asks, his voice strong and steady, he's been working up to this.

"Of course," I reply instantly. He's piqued my interest.

"I believe that security for your father, mother, stepmother, and step-sister need to be set up. We have no idea what Juan has planned or what he'll plan once Arturo is deported. We need to have every base covered."

I nod, "Okay, what is your plan?"

"How did you know that I have a plan already?"

I chuckle, "You wouldn't have approached this conversation without being thorough. So what is your plan?"

His back straightens as he glances in the rearview mirror, "I want to hire a few guys to come in and protect your family."

"Absolutely not." I don't trust newbies, hell I hardly trust my men. There's no way I'm hiring out for protection.

"Listen to me, Boss." He implores, "These guys, they're the best. They're not cops, and they don't belong to the government."

"So, who are they?" If they don't belong to the government, then who and what are they?

"They're a group of elite men and women. They've been in the military but now are their own company or should I say task force. Look I don't know much about them other than they're the best and they will make sure your family is safe."

He's not exactly making a good case for them. "That's all you got?"

He lets out a heavy sigh, "No, my brother Macka is part of the team. Boss, the only reason I even know about the team is because of Macka."

I frown, "I thought your brother died."

His smirk is reflected through the mirror, "Yeah, Boss; you're finally getting why they're the best."

It clicks, these men and women are supposedly dead; hence, they can do anything they want. "How long has this team been going? What do they specialize in?"

"Um..." He wavers, "That I'm not entirely sure of, I've not long found out he's still alive."

They're mercenaries, that's what they are. I'm not having anyone I don't know watch my family, but I'm not going to instantly dismiss it either. Martin brought it to me because he believes they would do a good job. I'm not going to cut down his idea, not just yet anyway.

"I'll let you know, in the meantime talk to Barney and let him know what the situation is. Tell him to keep his ear close to the ground. I'll be arriving there tonight, and I'll be bringing Jagger and you with me." I inform him, and he instantly nods. "It's my father's celebratory party for his marriage to Tina. I want everything to go smoothly."

"Yes Boss, I'll make sure that we're on top of things. I'll give Barney a call while you're in the meeting unless you need me to be present?"

"You can call Barney while Jagger and I have a meeting. Martin, as my second in command you are expected to be present at meetings, just as Jagger is." I probably should have let him know that I'd given him the title of second in command before today, but fuck it, this was as good as any other way.

"Of course, Boss." Pride in his voice, he understands the significance of being my second in command. I don't trust people, but those I do, I make sure they're close to me. Jagger was my best friend growing up, his mom is from the south, and Jagger has that southern drawl she had. Whereas his father, along with mine, started as my grandfather's soldiers before working their way up the ranks. Jagger's dad was shot dead by police believing he was robbing a store. He wasn't, and the officer who killed him almost five years ago now still is breathing. Something I plan on rectifying. Enough time has passed now that they won't automatically think it was us. Although suspicion will fall on us, it will look like an accident, one that happened while he was on the job.

"Martin, while we're in this meeting I need your

eyes on Matt and Carmine Jr. I don't trust those two." There's something about them that doesn't sit right with me, even when my dad was in charge. They're lazy, but they're slick too. They know too much for my liking.

"Funny you should mention those two. My gut screams every time those two schmucks are about."

He pulls up outside the new warehouse that Jagger had lined up for me. He'd been searching for a while and found three for us to use. He knows what I'm like, and he also knows that I'm cleaning house. But I'm going to try and control my temper and not kill anyone where I hold my meetings. Ending Ulric was my way of sending a message to the men that I don't give a fuck who I have to take out. If my men are behind me and loyal, they'll stay if they're not, they go.

Jagger's waiting outside for us, his posture is stiff, he's fucking pissed. I'm curious as to what Carina has done. Whatever it is, she's lucky to be alive. "They're all inside, the men are anxious, they're unsure of what you're planning on doing next."

I smirk, "It'll keep them on their toes. They now know not to fuck around and mess with me. I won't tolerate it."

He nods once and opens the door, as soon as I

walk in every single man stands to attention. Good, they've learned

"Cage what did you find about Detective Collins?" I get straight to the point as I walk towards them.

He takes a step forward, "Boss, I searched his place, he kept nothing of relevance there. I did some digging and found a storage container. He had files on you and your dad, but I've disposed of those. Stupid moron hadn't told anyone what Ulric had told him. So we're good." He puffs out his chest.

"How do you know that he hadn't told anyone?"

Darwin steps forward, a deep cough escaping him. "I may have taken his sister out for dinner."

Jesus.

He smirks, "She said that Collins didn't trust anyone on the force, he wasn't sure who you have in your pocket. So he was waiting until he had enough evidence to take to his superior."

"Thank fuck for his distrusting nature." Cage laughs, "Boss, everything is gone." he assures me.

I nod once, and they both step backward. "Matt and Carmine." My voice has taken on a dark edge.

They glance at each other, before hesitantly taking a step forward. "Yes, Boss?"

"Where is Ulric's body?" He hasn't been found yet, and I'm curious as to where they've dumped him.

Matt stands taller, "There's a new mall going up in Barstow, they laid the foundation for it this morning. Ulric is about ten feet underneath that foundation."

"Good." I nod to them, and they take a step backward.

"There's been a threat made against my family. I'll be staying close this weekend. Make sure you are by your phones. I don't care what you are doing, I call, you drop whatever it is, and you come. Do you understand?"

"Yes, Boss." They say in unison.

"You're dismissed." One by one, they leave the warehouse, each of them wanting to leave as soon as possible in case I change my mind. "Martin," I call as Darwin and Cage leave. "Follow those two assholes Matt and Carmine Jr and see where they go. I don't buy what they said. Have Sam find any evidence of this happening. They drove to Barstow, there's going to be a trail. Find it."

"On it, call me when you're ready to leave, it's a five-hour journey to go to your father's."

I laugh, "We're not driving. We're taking the

chopper. We're leaving at five. Make sure your bags are packed, and you're ready to go by then."

He nods and leaves the warehouse, leaving Jagger and I alone.

"What did Carina do?"

He hands me his phone, and I glance at the screen. It's an email. "I received this today." Each word vibrating with anger.

I have to read the email twice to make sure that I read it right. Holy fuck, what the hell did I just read?

"Jag?" I say through gritted teeth, "Want to tell me why it says that you told her you didn't want the baby?"

His eyes flash with anger. "Those words never left my mouth. Up until this email, I had no idea that Sarah was pregnant." His breathing is hard, his chest rising and falling, I've never seen him this mad before.

"Fuck, Jag." I stare at the picture of the little girl, a cute smile on her face, her blue eyes are bright like the sea, and she has one tiny tooth. "This is your daughter man; there's no denying that fucking smile."

"I have a child, one that was kept from me." He shouts. "She kept my child from me, Hudson."

"You need to calm the fuck down," I warn him. He's mad but at the wrong damn person. "Did you read the email? Or did you see the picture and see that you have a child?"

His nostrils flare. "Hudson..."

I shake my head and hand him his phone, "Don't Hudson me anything Jag. Read the fucking email. Out loud."

He snatches the cell out of my hand, "Jagger," He begins, "I know you said that you didn't want the baby and I completely understand that, it's your right not to be involved if you don't want to." Tears shine in his eyes. I don't say anything and let him continue. "I attached a picture of Allie, and I want you to know that you have a daughter, if you ever change your mind about wanting to know her, please don't hesitate to get in contact. I hope you're well Jag, and I pray that you change your mind. All my love, Sarah."

"Tell me something Jag, does that sound like a woman who kept your child from you?" I ask him after a couple of minutes, once he's managed to get himself under control.

He jerks his head, "No," he growls.

I nod. "Okay, what's your plan?"

He throws his hands in the air, "I have no

fucking idea, I have no clue where she is. I want my daughter."

"Your daughter has a mother. She's not just going to hand her over to you Jag." I'm trying to be the voice of reason to him. I know that he wants his baby, I would too if I was in his position, but he needs to go about this the right way.

"I want them both. Fuck Hudson, you know that I've wanted Sarah."

I smirk, "I know, so you send her an email, telling her you need to talk. Find out what happened. Why she believes that you didn't want Allie in the first place. Something happened to make her think that way, and you need to find out what."

He nods, "I'll email her on the way to your dad's, I need to think out a response. Right now, I can't think of what to say."

"That's a good idea," I have a feeling I know where Sarah got the idea that Jag didn't want the baby, Carina. That bitch has to have had something to do with this. "I'm proud of you Jag. You didn't call her and demand answers."

He chuckles, "Who would have thought it, huh? That the two of us would think before we act?"

I flip him off as I walk out of the warehouse, "You're driving, I need to get shit sorted before we leave." I couldn't care less about this stupid fucking party, but I gave him my word. I never go back on my word. Ever.

Walking into Dad's house I already want to leave, it's filled with pretentious people and I'm being watched like a hawk as I move into the ballroom. My dad has his arm around Tina's waist, a smile on his face. He looks happier than I have ever seen him, but it pisses me off. He treats Tina with love and respect. Buys her this house like it's nothing and yet my mom's living in squalor in comparison, it shouldn't be like that.

My eyes glance around the room, taking in everyone who's here, women bat their lashes at me or flash me a come hither smile. I ignore them. I'm not here for a hookup.

"Uh, Boss," Jagger says, and I face him, his nostrils flaring again, great what the fuck is up now? "You may want to look to your right." He instructs me.

I do, my eyes glance to my right, in the corner of the room is the raven-haired goddess that I spent the night with almost two years ago. The woman that came apart in my arms and I watched because she was fucking magnificent is staring back at me with her mouth parted in surprise. The red-haired woman beside her whispers something to her and her complexion pales.

"Ah, Hudson, there you are." Dad's voice calls out, and I manage to pull my eyes away from the beauty and look at him. "Hudson this is Tina,"

Tina walks over to me and pulls me into her arms, "It's such a pleasure to meet you, Hudson, your father has told me so much about you. You don't understand how much I've been wanting to meet you." She's rambling. It's irritating as she keeps glancing toward my dad, she's frightened of me.

"Tina, it's nice to meet you too," I tell her as I pull away from her.

She smiles brightly at me, as she pushes her blonde hair behind her shoulder, "Oh, you have to meet Mia." She says excitedly, and I inwardly groan. I've not met my step-sister yet, but I'm dreading it. "Darling have you seen where Mia's disappeared to?"

My dad smirks, "Ah, she's hiding in the corner, although I'm wondering who gave her that glass of champagne."

Tina gasps, "She's not old enough to drink, oh great, Lacey's doing it too." I watch in amusement as she storms off ahead of us.

"Tina's a bit protective of Mia." Dad explains.

"Oh shit," Jagger says, and I follow his line of sight to see Tina talking to the raven-haired beauty.

"Hudson." Tina says as I approach her, "Meet Mia, your new sister."

Oh fuck, this isn't good. I'm already fucking hard from thinking about the way she wrapped those perfectly plump lips around my dick. I won't be able to keep away from her. I already want her again.

Something flashes in Mia's eyes as she looks at Jagger, "He's not my brother." She says in disgust, "If you'll excuse me, I need to use the ladies room." She walks away from us, her friend rushing behind her.

"Mia, what happened?" Her friend asks, and that's what I'd like to know.

"That asshole beside Hudson? That's Jagger. I need to get away before I rip his balls off." She murmurs, and I can't help but smile as I watch

Jagger wince. Damn it though, hearing her feisty side doesn't help my dick. I want her more than I've ever wanted another woman.

EIGHT

Mia

"Shit, Mia, what are you going to do?" Lacey questions as I pull her up the stairs behind me, I'm trying to escape, I need to get away.

Firstly, Jagger's here. The man that hurt my friend more than any of her mom's boyfriends and husbands could have. Secondly, Hudson is the man I've spent the best part of two years fantasizing about. Now I find out he's my stepbrother. I'm totally screwed.

"I don't know, but I need to call Sarah, she needs to know that Jagger's here."

"My room, we'll Facetime her." She tells me and pulls me into her room with her. She immediately powers on the laptop that's on the dressing table.

Sarah answers, with Allie in her arms and she's

sporting a huge smile on her face. "This is a pleasant surprise. You both look gorgeous. Although not very original. Surely there were other colors besides black? How's the party going?"

"Black is slimming." Lacey informs her, "The party is a drag. I've never been so bored in my life."

"Mia, is everything okay?" Sarah frowns as she looks at me.

I shake my head, "He's here Sarah, Jagger's here."

Sarah's face slackens, she looks to be in shock. Allie begins to cry, probably feeling her mother's emotions.

"He's here Sarah, I had to walk away; otherwise I was going to say and do something to him. I just want to punch him." I tell her and watch as she soothes Allie in her arms.

"Did he reply to your email?" Lacey asks, and I feel like shit for not asking her that.

She finally manages to get Allie to settle, "No, he hasn't, not that I really expected him to. Look, don't mention me or Allie while you're around him. What is he doing there anyway? Does he know your stepdad?"

Lacey begins to laugh, and I elbow her to stop,

it's not funny. Having just found out that Hudson is my stepbrother has knocked me for six.

"Okay, spill," Sarah demands but she's cut off by the bedroom door opening.

"Mia, you were extremely rude," Mom says as she walks into Lacey's room, she looks at the computer screen and gasps. "Sarah."

Sarah gives Mom a smile and a little wave, "Hey, Mrs. Brady. Congratulations, I hope you and Mr. Brady are very happy together." She says ignoring Mom's shocked expression.

"Mom, knock much?" I know she's pissed that I was rude, but this is Lacey's room and she shouldn't walk in without knocking.

She coughs, unable to take her eyes off Sarah and Allie. "I apologize Lacey, but Mia, how dare you?"

"What happened?" Sarah inquires looking between us all.

Mom's standing with her arms crossed, and now she begins to tap her foot. "Mia met her stepbrother and his friend." She begins, "She decided that she'd be rude by telling us that Hudson wasn't her brother and walking away without saying hello. Mia, that was a really immature thing to do."

"His friend is Jagger," Lacey informs Sarah, and her face immediately hardens.

"Am I missing something?" Mom asks as she looks between all three of us. "Someone better start talking."

I sigh and walk toward the open door, "Let me shut and lock the door. We don't need anyone else barging in on us."

"Okay Mrs. Brady, you're not going to like what we have to say, and I apologize for that." Sarah begins.

"What did you do?" Mom asks as she sits on the bed.

I glance at the computer screen and see Sarah glancing down at Allie. Great, it's up to me to tell her. "Do you remember the night before we left?"

Mom's eyes narrow, "You stayed at Sarah's, didn't you?"

"No, we rented out a motel, and we went to a nightclub," I tell her, but I feel bad for deceiving her. She truly believed that I was at Sarah's that night.

"I met a man and we hit it off, I went home with him." Sarah shrugs, she sounds as though it doesn't faze her when we all know that's not the case. "Silly huh, a one night stand results in this beautiful baby." Her voice goes soft when she talks about Allie; her eyes are so full of love as she looks at her daughter. "I'm sorry that we lied to you Mrs. Brady, but we wanted to celebrate finishing school. We had such a blast."

Mom's silent for what feels like ages, "Do you know what could have happened to you? I can't believe how irresponsible you both were. Sarah, have you been in contact with the baby's father?"

I watch as Sarah's spine straightens. "Mrs. Brady, how long have you known me? Do you really think I'd keep my child from her father?"

Mom stares at her, "I didn't think you'd put yourself in danger by going to a club. Underage I may add."

Sarah doesn't back down. "Look Mrs. Brady, both Mia and I regret lying to you. We don't regret going out. We had fun, something we needed after a shit year with school. To answer your question, I went to see him the next day before I left for New York, he had gotten back with his ex. I called him when I found out I was pregnant, he didn't answer, so I left a message asking for him to call me back. He didn't. He got his girlfriend to call me instead."

Mom's eyes fill with tears, "Oh, Sarah."

Sarah's not finished yet. "She told me that he

didn't want our baby and to never contact him or them again. I didn't, not until today when I sent him an email letting him know that if he ever changed his mind about Allie that she'd love to meet him. He hasn't responded."

Mom's eyes flash with anger. "Who is he?"

"Jagger." I whisper, and she gasps, "That's why I was rude. I couldn't stand there and be nice Mom. He hurt Sarah, and he's hurting Allie by not being there. I'm sorry."

She waves her hand, "I understand why now." She stands, "Sarah, you ever need anything, please let me know, I don't care what it is, if I can help, I will."

Sarah smiles, "Thank you Mrs. Brady. Please don't say anything to anyone. I've not told my mom yet. I'm not sure I want Allie around her. I don't trust her. She's not changed, she'll never change. You know that Mrs. Brady."

"I won't say a word. Thank you for letting me know. Girls, come downstairs when you're ready." She says as she places a kiss on my cheek. I walk with her to the door and unlock it so that she can leave. "I understand why you did it. I'm just upset that you felt the need to lie to me. Why wouldn't you tell me? It's not like you to keep secrets from me, Mia."

I can't help the irony of her words, "We've both kept secrets haven't we Mom? I mean, you didn't tell me you were engaged, nor did you tell me you were married until a few days after it happened. Don't be a hypocrite..." Mom's eyes flash with hurt at my words, and I instantly feel bad, "What Sarah and I did is what every young person does. We went out and had fun, we were wrong to lie to you, but it's done now."

She gingerly reaches out and touches my cheek. "You've been hurt so much, and I never wanted to add any more to you."

It makes sense now. I couldn't understand why she never told me about her and Harrison. "You thought I'd be hurt that you were moving on?"

She nods as tears spring to her eyes, "Mia, you were a daddy's girl, you had been from the moment you were born, as soon as he held you he told me that the world had finally made sense. I completely understood how he felt. We both loved you deeply; I still do. But you and your dad were always closer than you and I ever were, and when he died you pulled away. I could never reach you." Her voice is barely a whisper as a lone tear falls down her face.

"You were hurting, and I couldn't help you. I had no idea how I could stop your pain."

"I miss him, Mom. I thought you were trying to wipe away every remnant of him and the life you shared with him." God, this isn't the time to be having this discussion, not now, not at her party.

She pulls me into her arms, "Mia, your father was a big part of my life. I loved him with every fiber of my being. I still love him, had he not died we would have grown old together and lived a very happy life. I'm so sorry that you thought I was doing that."

My arms tighten around her, and I squeeze her tightly, "I love you, Mom. I'm sorry for being rude."

She pulls away from me, her hands going to my face. "Don't be sorry, I completely understand why you did it, but Mia, Jagger is Hudson's best friend which means he's going to be around a lot while they're here. You're going to have to be civil. For the sake of Sarah and Allie, you have to be. He's made his decision, one that none of us agree with. But his none the less"

I groan, "I know, I'm going to have to try and bite my tongue."

She laughs, "I know you will baby, Sarah and Allie don't need the stress. I'd better get back downstairs. Say goodbye to them and come down when you're ready."

"I will do Mom, thanks for listening."

Her face softens, "Always."

When she starts to go down the stairs, I turn and close the door, "Sorry, we couldn't help but overhear." Lacey tells me as I turn to face them.

I shake my head, "You didn't even try, did you?" They both smile, "No, okay ladies, I have got to go, I need to change Allie, and get some dinner for the both of us."

"Okay, call if you need us," I tell her, even though I know she won't, she never will. She's determined to do this all by herself.

"I will. Try not to let Jagger get to you. He's actually a really sweet guy, and you'd like him if you got to know him."

Lacey's mouth drops open in surprise, whereas I'm not even surprised, she's always said Jagger was a good guy, he just doesn't want a baby. "Go, and feed that gorgeous goddaughter of mine."

Lacey pushes my shoulder, "No, she's mine."

Sarah just shakes her head. It's something we always argue about. Sarah is undecided if she's going to baptize Allie, it doesn't matter I'm still her auntie. "Have fun at the party girls and if it gets that boring, why not go back to Oakland for a bit?"

"Not a bad idea," I tell her, actually contemplating going back home, maybe to look at the old house, it's not sold yet so I could spend a night or two there. I actually like that idea. I could feel a bit closer to Dad, go and visit his grave.

Allie's face gets bright red, and she makes a weird, but telling sound that we've all heard before. I laugh, "We'll let you go and deal with that."

Sarah groans, "I'm going to need a gas mask, how can a small child's poop smell so bad? Okay, call me soon."

I blow her a kiss, "Will do. Bye, love you both."

"Bye ladies, love you." She calls out and ends the call.

Lacey huffs out a breath, "God, we should move to New York. I feel so helpless, she's slaying this whole mother thing though. I want to help her as much as I can, even though she won't let us help her."

"I know, but Sarah wouldn't let us. She wants us to do what we've dreamed of. So we do whatever we can do. I'm going to talk to Mom and see if there's anything we can do to help, even though she won't accept anything, Mom can be persuasive so she'll help us." It feels good having her know, I can talk to her about it now, and the frustrations I'm feeling about her struggling.

"Sounds good. Now, are you ready to go back down there?"

I shrug, "I guess so." I don't really have much of a choice.

"What are you going to do about Hudson?"

"Ugh, can we deal with one thing at a time?" I ask, not wanting to think about him or what effect he has on my body.

She smirks, "Sure, although I doubt he's going to leave it alone."

I roll my eyes, "I doubt he even remembers me." I link my arm through hers, "Let's rejoin the party. I need a drink."

She laughs, "Or two? Can we hide out in the garden?"

"Definitely," I tell her as we leave her room, "What about you and Barney?"

"What about us?" She's avoiding, and I want to know why, but as soon as we begin to descend the stairs both Hudson and Jagger are at the bottom along with some other man that I don't know.

I pull my arm from Lacey's and straighten my spine, "I'm sorry for my rudeness." I say looking directly at Hudson. I watch as his lips twitch, "I'm not usually that rude."

"It's true. She's usually sweet." Lacey chimes in.

"Oh, I know." Hudson replies and Lacey laughs, he knows who I am. Fuck.

"Mia." Jagger says, and I look to him, "Do you think that we'll be able to talk?"

I shrug, "Sure," I say as I come to stand beside him and Hudson. I wonder what he wants to talk about, if he even mentions Sarah or Allie, I'm going to walk away.

"Outside?" Hudson barks and I jump. "Sorry." He whispers as he looks down at me, his hand grazing my back.

Goosebumps break out on my skin, and I'm transported back to twenty months ago. The magnetic feeling I had is back, I'm drawn to him, and I shouldn't be, I need to get my head together, Hudson Brady is someone I can't be attracted to.

"Uh, yeah, give me a minute, I just want to get a drink," I tell them while grabbing a hold of Lacey's hand and pulling her with me into the ballroom. "Shit Lace, what am I meant to do?"

"Oh, Mia, you still like him, don't you?" She puts her arm around my shoulder as we make our way through the ballroom and towards the kitchen.

"Like?" I scoff, "It's so much more than that. That night we spent together, it's all I ever think about. It's pathetic I know, but Lace, he's all I have ever wanted." Now, I can't have him.

"Damn, Mia," Lacey exclaims, "You never said you loved him."

I come to a stop as we walk through the kitchen doors. Turning to face her. I raise my hands, "Whoa, who mentioned anything about love?"

She has this annoying look on her face, the one that tells me she knows more than I do. I roll my eyes and pull my phone out of the pocket I have hidden in my dress. I quickly send Sarah a text.

Jagger wants to speak to me, what if he wants to talk about you and Allie? Do I talk to him, or do I ignore him?

She doesn't take long to message me back.

You can speak to him, I have nothing to hide. Maybe you can get him to understand that he's hurting his daughter

with his decision. Let me know how it goes, try not to kill him. Love you Mia, thank you for being here for me. I don't know what I'd have done without you.

God, she's trying to make me cry! Taking a deep breath, I put my cell back into my pocket and spy the bottles of champagne and a few glasses. Shrugging, I pick the glasses up, Lacey grabs the bottle, and we make our way out into the back yard, it's freaking huge. I spot Hudson and Jagger in mid discussion, so I make my way over to the patio set Mom has out here. Taking a seat I place the glasses on the table.

"Hey, relax okay, if things get heated, just walk away. You owe neither of them anything." Lacey says as she reaches out and touches my hand.

"I know, I just want him to realize what he's actually missing out on not being around Allie. He's hurt Sarah so much by just being an asshole. I don't want to make things worse for them, I know how mad I am at him and I'm trying my hardest to be calm and talk to him like a normal person, but all I keep seeing is Allie in my head. I hate it, Lace. I hate him." My voice cracks and a tear slowly falls down my face as I peer over at him and Hudson, they're still talking, Jagger has a smile on his face. "My best friend is struggling, and he's here having the fucking time of his life. It makes me sick."

She squeezes my hand, "Deep breath, Mia. You've got this. You're a fucking amazing friend, you'd go to hell and back for us, and that's why we love you. Your loyalty is outstanding."

I shrug, I'd do what they'd do for me. It's what you do for those who you love.

"Thank you Mia," Jagger says softly as he and Hudson come and sit down beside us, of course Hudson takes the seat beside me.

"Hudson, Jagger, this is Lacey, Lacey, meet Hudson and Jagger." I introduce them, and Lacey doesn't shake either of their hands. Instead, she just gives them a soft wave. "You wanted to talk?" I get straight to the point.

He nods, "Yes, I received an email today, and it knocked me for six..." He begins, his hands flat against the table.

I scoff, "Why, because you thought she'd have gotten rid of it?"

His eyes widen before quickly darkening. His nostrils flare, and his hands ball up into a fist. "No,

God, no. What the fuck? Mia, this email is the first I ever knew about having a daughter."

I gasp, what? There's no way. I glance at Lacey. She looks as shocked as I feel.

"Mia, please, tell me what the fuck is going on," Jagger begs me.

"From the beginning, please. " Hudson asks, his hand reaching over and touching my leg, I should push it away, but I don't. Instead, I hold onto it as if it's my lifeline. He entwines our fingers together, and a sense of calm settles over me. Shit, I am so screwed.

"Okay, where do I start?" I don't know how much he knows.

"You both left without a word." Hudson's deep voice sends shivers down my back, "Why?"

"It wasn't planned. Sarah and I went out that night. We wanted to let off steam. We were both leaving Oakland, and neither of us could wait. The further away we got the better." I tell them honestly, and Hudson's hand tightens around mine. "We went out and we wanted to have fun. We did, and you and Jagger, you weren't expected." I tell him, needing him to understand that it wasn't a plan we had come up with. It just happened.

"Jagger, you were with Carina that night. Sarah

thought you two had gotten back together, but at the end of the night when you had asked her to go home with you, she did because she trusted you." I shake my head, "That was her very first mistake."

I watch as he flinches, I don't mean it to hurt him, I'm just telling him the truth.

"My cell ringing woke me up," I tell Hudson, my eyes looking into his, "I had to go, I didn't want to wake you. You looked so peaceful. I thought it would be better to just leave without saying goodbye." More so for me because that one night meant so much more for me than I had ever anticipated.

Looking back at Jagger I see he's waiting patiently for me to continue, "So Sarah and I met up and we headed back to Oakland, we went to our homes and packed up our cars before meeting one last time, she told me she was going back to find you, to talk to you. Tell you where she was headed, and you could hit her up if you were in the area."

"She didn't though," his voice hoarse as he blinks, almost as if he's trying to make sense of what happened.

I shake my head, "That was Sarah's second mistake. She arrived outside your house only to see you and Carina making out, so she drove and she continued until she got the hell out of Cali."

I can't believe I'm telling him this. He should know this. What if he doesn't? It would change everything.

NINE

Hudson

"Fuck." Jagger's words are guttural, he fucked up, and he knows it. What the fuck was he doing making out with that bitch mere hours after being with Sarah?

"Sarah found out she was pregnant when she was about eight or nine weeks. She contemplated whether or not she was going to keep it." Mia's voice is soft and willowy, and her hand is gripped tight in mine, I thought she'd ignore it when I reached over and touched her thigh, she shocked me by taking my hand into hers, she's held on tightly ever since. The woman is making my head spin, I want her and I shouldn't but fuck, she's mine, and I'm not going to stop until she's in my bed.

Permanently. She was mine before our parents got married. I don't care if we're family now.

"What?" Jagger shouts and both Mia and Lacey jump.

Before I'm able to reprimand him, Mia stands up, her hand pulling away from mine and she leans over the table. Her finger pointing in his face. "Don't you dare. Don't even think about making it about that. She had no one, Jagger. Sarah lives alone, she's in a new fucking city and has no friends, the man who got her pregnant didn't give a fuck about her and not even six hours after her leaving his bed he's making out with someone else. Don't you dare sit there and get mad that she contemplated an abortion."

He nods, his eyes so full of pain. I've never seen him look so defeated. He's kicking himself for letting her get away.

"She decided that she couldn't do it, that she'd be a single mom and fuck she's amazing. I'm in awe of her. Allie has the best mom in the world." Tears fall from her eyes as she sits back down. "Sarah loves her more than anything. You can't blame her for thinking through all her options."

"You're right. I'm not angry. I'm actually really proud of how she managed to think things out. I would have understood had she had an abortion." He tells her and I don't believe him. He'd be a fucker, he'd do everything in his power to destroy her for killing his kid. How do I know this? Jagger and I are the same, and if a woman did that to my child, I'd make her suffer.

"She contemplated telling you, she wanted you to know, but she didn't want to make things between you and Carina difficult." Yeah, she doesn't like that bitch either. "She'd landed her dream job even though she was pregnant, she thought you deserved to know the truth, so she did the one thing she promised herself she'd never do. She returned to Cali, back to Synergy. You were with Carina. She said you looked happy and she couldn't bring herself to tell you then and there, so she called you, left a message asking you to call her back. That was her third mistake."

Jagger frowns, "I never got a call, hell I never got a message. I would have called her back!"

Mia shrugs, "Well Sarah got a call back. Not from you, but she did get a call back telling her that you didn't want the baby and to leave you alone and to never contact you again. Sarah never mentioned her pregnancy on the voice message she left." She swallows harshly, "Her fourth mistake was listening to me. I told her to send you the email. I didn't think you'd be a heartless bastard and ignore it." She shakes her head looking at him in disgust.

I reach for her hand, and she instantly looks at me, "Who called her Mia?"

More tears fall, her eyelashes are wet, "Carina." She confesses, and the mood around the table immediately shifts. That bitch is dead. I don't give a shit, she's fucked, and I'm going to make sure she has a painful fucking death.

"Why?" Jagger's voice cracks and my best friend, the man who doesn't bat a fucking eyelid as he guts someone, chokes up. "Why would she do this, how the fuck did she do this?" He asks as he finally manages to compose himself.

"She must have seen Sarah at Synergy when she was pregnant and intercepted the message," Lacey speaks up as the little redhead reaches for the bottle of champagne and pours us all glasses. "Question that I have is why haven't you replied to Sarah?"

I take a glass from her and own up. "That would be down to me. See, Jag and I have a penchant for being hotheads, and I told him not to. He needed to think before he acted, he thought that Sarah had kept Allie away from him and he was mad as hell."

"Typical man," Mia mutters as she brings her glass to her lips.

"So what are you going to do now that you know the truth?" Lacey asks.

"I'm going to spend my life making it up to both Sarah and Allie." Jagger instantly replies, not even thinking about it.

"Who said that Sarah wants you?" Mia raises her eyebrow at him, and she's a pitbull when she needs to be. Fuck, I'd hate to be on the wrong side of her.

Jagger smirks, and I know that he loves a challenge. He's not going to stop until he has Sarah just as I won't until I have Mia. "Where is she?" he asks, and both girls sit back in their chairs and don't say a word. "Mia, Lacey, please." He pleads with them.

Mia shakes her head. "Look, I've told you everything that's happened. There's one person who you owe an apology to. She gave you a way of contacting her. You're just being an ass now, demanding we tell you where she is. I'm never going to tell you so why don't you pick up that fancy ass phone of yours and email her back?" Her smile is triumphant as she takes another sip of champagne.

"Right, thanks. I'm going. I'll call you tomorrow." He says, getting to his feet.

"Oh, Jagger." Mia calls out sweetly, and he stops in his tracks, turning to look at her, "Hurt her or Allie again and I swear I'll hurt you so bad you won't be able to walk for a week. Do you understand?" Such venom for such a little lady.

Jagger glances at me and smirks. Yeah, I'm going to have fun with Mia.

"I won't." He assures her, "That's my daughter, and I'm going to make sure that nothing ever hurts her. Thank you for looking after them for me."

"Fuck," Mia whispers as she wipes tears from her eyes. "The asshole had to say that! I was fine hating him and then he comes out with that."

Lacey laughs, but she too has tears in her eyes. "I'll be back later, I need to make a phone call."

Mia's eyes widen before she slowly smiles, "Okay," and it's in that moment that I realize Lacey's going to call Sarah and let her know what's happened. I should stop them, but I don't. They've looked after their friend when Jagger couldn't, and they're protecting her, making sure she's not blindsided.

"You left," I say when Lacey leaves us alone.

She stands and turns her chair around so that

she's facing me properly. She sits back down; I do the same. She's even more beautiful than I remember. What nobody knows, not even Jagger is that Mia has ruined me. I've not slept with anyone since her. I've been searching for her for a long time, and she's finally here. We're in a fucked-up situation, but that's not going to stop me from having her. She's mine, and I plan on keeping her that way forever.

"I'm sorry, I know that I should have left a note or something. I didn't think you'd want to hear from me again." Her voice is gentle as she wrings her hands together.

"Mia, you were a virgin, why me?" It's something that's been playing on my mind since that night, I knew as soon as I entered her that she was innocent and I should have pulled out and walked away but I couldn't, as soon as I thrust inside of her, she was mine.

She blushes, her porcelain skin turning bright red. "I didn't think you noticed."

I take her hand and pull her toward me, she comes a little hesitantly, but as soon as she sits on my lap, she softens against me. "Mia, you never did answer me, why me?" I whisper.

She sighs, "I don't know Hudson, there's

something about you that I can't explain. You make me feel things that I've never felt before. It's like you're a magnet, I'm being sucked into you and no matter how much I resist it doesn't work." Her voice is a whisper and it hits me in the gut. She feels this pull too, that's good, because it means I won't have to work too hard at persuading her.

"Mia, I'm not a good man. I'm never going to be one either." I won't do what my dad did; it's not who I am. I wouldn't turn my back on that life, it's in my blood. "I can't promise the future, but I can promise that I will make you feel like the princess you are."

Her breath hitches, "Hudson." She whispers and fuck, she needs to stop. My dick is hard enough to cut diamonds. "We can't do this, you're my stepbrother."

I turn her around so that she's straddling me, such sadness etched on her face. "I don't give a fuck. You're mine, Mia, and no one is going to deny me what's mine." I growl as I capture her mouth kissing her hard and fast. Fuck, how can I have missed her when I only spent one night with her?

She whimpers as I pull away, "Hudson, we can't." She gets up off my lap and walks over to her chair, "I'm sorry."

I smile, she's so fucking polite. "Why are you apologizing?"

Tears swim in her eyes, "Because I don't want to hurt you."

So fucking innocent.

"Mia, you're not hurting me." I tell her truthfully, "This thing between us, it's never going to go away. You've been on my mind for almost two years now. I know what I want, do you believe that because our parents are married that it's going to end whatever this is?"

"They won't like it." She tells me, and I know right there that she wants this as much as I do.

"Baby, you leave them to me. Okay?"

She bites her lip, her eyes glance to the ground, she's unsure. "Hudson..."

"Boss." Martin's voice calls out and Mia immediately straightens, she's frowning as she looks between Martin and I.

"Yes?" My irritation clear, whatever it is had better be life or death.

"Um, Boss," he says again looking extremely uncomfortable, good the fucker, he may have undone all the work I laid out tonight.

"I'll be back in a minute," I tell her and I can tell from the glassy eyes that she's already gone back to the woman who doesn't believe we should be doing this. "What?" I growl as I come to stand in front of Martin.

He doesn't react to my annoyance, "Boss, Arturo has been arrested. I've been told on good authority that he'll be deported within the week."

"Week?"

Martin sighs, "Boss, they can't just deport someone, they have to go through the proper channels. It'll be done."

Fuck. "Fine, what about that asshole Juan? What's he doing?"

"He's pissed. Jorge said that he doesn't suspect that he was set up, which gives us the element of surprise in whatever it is you have planned." He smiles, "Boss, do you need me to stay around?"

"No, you can leave. Let me know if there's any more updates." I peer into the house. It doesn't seem as though anyone has left yet. Great, no way to escape, without having a lecture about it.

He nods, "Will do, Barney's here if you need him. If you can pry him away from the redhead."

I smirk, I knew as soon as I saw Lacey that she'd be Barney's type. "Thanks, Martin." I turn and head back toward Mia.

Just as I sit down the door opens again, and

Lacey barrels through it. "He's an asshole Mia." She practically growls as she sits down.

Mia smirks, "What's he done now?"

Lacey reaches for the bottle of champagne and fills her glass as Barney comes outside. "The jerk asked me if I wanted to go home with him. I mean what type of woman does he take me for? Who really goes home with someone they don't know because they growl and shit?"

Mia blushes, and I smirk. That's exactly how it happened with us. I still don't understand how a sweet virgin went home with me that night but fuck, I'm glad she did.

Lacey gasps as she takes in Mia's beet-red face and my smirk, "No offense, Mia."

Mia shrugs, "I don't regret it. It was amazing. But Lacey, if you don't want to, then don't."

"I don't give up that easily Red," Barney grins as he joins us at the table. "You playing hard to get is just making me hard."

I shake my head, what an ass.

Lacey looks at him in disgust. "Pig."

Mia's trying hard not to laugh, "Sorry Barney, that doesn't work on Lacey. You want her, you're going to have to come up with something better than your caveman act."

Barney slams his hand on the table, "Challenge accepted."

Lacey's eyes widen, "Whoa." She says, raising her hands in the air, "Nobody said anything about a challenge. I don't accept a challenge."

Mia laughs, and I catch her mouthing the word 'Liar' to Lacey, I don't get the whole playing hard to get. It's a complete turn-off, if you're into each other go for it. Mia's not playing hard to get with me. She's confused, and I just need to clear her head of any confusion.

The back door opens and Dad and Tina walk out, both of them with wide smiles. Tina's head rests against his shoulder, his arm around her, holding her close to him. He was never this intimate with Mom, he was an asshole toward her, and I hated him

"I'm so glad you're all getting along." Tina looks at Mia with such softness.

"Bored, Mom?" Mia asks with a smile making both Lacey and my dad laugh.

Tina's eyes widen, "Why would you say that?"

Mia cocks one perfectly shaped brow, "Oh, besides the fact that you've come outside and left your hundreds of guests inside, it could be the fact that as soon as you escaped..."

Tina gasps, "I did not escape."

"Suuureee." Mia says, "As I was saying, as soon as you escaped you look relieved."

Lacey hoots, "She's right, Mrs. Brady, I don't think I've ever seen you look so relieved."

Tina waves her hands, "Oh hush up, you two. What am I going to do with you?"

"Do you have any plans while you girls are here?" Dad asks, he seems so at ease around them, I feel like I'm in the Twilight Zone or some shit, he's different. I'm not sure what to make of it.

Mia glances at her hands, she's nervous, I want to reach out and pull her toward me, but I know that she'd be pissed if I did that. I need to get her used to it first before I do it.

"Um Mom, do you still have the keys to the old house?" Mia's voice is hesitant.

"Yes, do you want to go back?" Tina stares at her, and it's as if they're having a silent conversation.

Mia nods, "Yeah, after what we were talking about earlier, it would be nice. While I'm here, I want to go visit Dad."

I frown, her dad? I wonder where he is. My dad hasn't mentioned him at all.

"Of course, do you want me to come with you? We can go to the grave together?"

Grave? Shit, her dad must be dead.

Mia stands, tears swimming in her eyes, "No, I've not been in a while. I'll be okay."

Dad pulls Tina closer, offering her support. "I'll give you the keys tomorrow, when are you thinking of going?"

Mia shrugs, "I don't know yet. I'm tired, I'm going to call it a night."

Dad pulls Mia into his arms, her entire body is tight. Whatever he whispers to her eases her slightly, and my fists ball. Great, I'm jealous of my dad. Fuck. Dad releases her and Tina pulls her into her arms.

"Of course, rest, we'll talk tomorrow. This party is over anyway; everyone's getting ready to leave. It's almost one am," Tina presses a kiss against Mia's temple. "I love you, Mia."

"I love you too Mom,"

I stand, "I'm going to go too, I've a bit of work to do before I call it a night."

"Son, there's a room here for you," Dad tells me with a smile, "Mia, will you show Hudson his room, your room is beside his."

"Sure, Lace, you staying here or you going to bed?" Mia asks as she glances at me.

Lacey glances at Barney, "I'm going to bed." She stands up, not before giving Barney a filthy look.

"Barney dear, would you like me to set up the spare room for you?" Tina asks, and Barney's eyes widen in shock. He's an employee and Tina's treating him as though he's family.

"Um, Mrs. Brady that would be great but no need to go to any trouble. If you point me in the right direction, I'll make the bed."

Lacey walks toward Tina, quickly glancing over her shoulder at Barney. "I'll show you, Mrs. Brady showed me earlier. Goodnight Mrs. and Mr. Brady, thank you for a wonderful evening. The party was..." She pauses as she glances at Mia, "Delightful."

Tina laughs, "You're sweet and full of shit, you and Mia hid for the entire evening. Ladies, you aren't even twenty yet, no more drinking."

"Wait, what?" I say a little too loudly, making both Tina and my dad look over at me. I compose myself and think on my feet. "You've been in my club." I give her a pointed look.

"Hudson?" Dad questions, "How did she get in? When did she get in?"

I give him a look, "That's what I'd like to know."

Mia's eyes are wide, "Mia went to the club almost two years ago, not long after her eighteenth birthday." Tina's tone is full of disapproval. "I have no idea how she and Sarah ended up in your club, although now isn't the time to discuss this."

"Not the time to discuss this? She got into my club underage. If the cops found out about this shit, I could be shut down." I growl, I've got the cops on my ass enough as it is, if they think kids are getting into my club, they'll be on me even more. "Who was on the door?" I ask Mia and her eyes flash with anger.

"Hudson, just make sure it doesn't happen again."

I grind my teeth at his words. I know how to run my own damn club. I'll be making sure this shit doesn't happen again.

Mia shrugs, "How am I supposed to know who was on the door, I only went once. Anyway, I'm going to bed." She's pissed, and I don't blame her I'm acting like an ass, although I've just found out I fucked her when she was barely eighteen, I was twenty-six. Shit, at least she was legal.

I follow her into the house. She's walking fast, probably trying to get away from me. "Mia," I call as she begins walking up the stairs.

"What Hudson?" She asks, sounding resigned.

"I'm sorry, I was an ass."

Her eyebrows raise in surprise, "Wow, didn't expect that."

I smirk, "I can apologize when I need to, but Mia, I was shocked, I didn't realize that you were so young."

She shrugs, and it pisses me off, "It's over and done with Hudson, you don't need to worry about me being so young." Hurt in each and every single word she says.

I don't say anything until we reach the top floor, "That's your room." She points to the door on the left.

I grab her arm as she walks towards her room and pull her back to me, her body crashing against mine. "Mia, I don't give a fuck how old you are. I was shocked, but relieved you were legal."

She rolls her eyes, "Oh, and if I wasn't?"

"I would have to wait," I growl, my dick hard as fucking stone.

"For what?"

I smirk, "You to become legal. You're mine,

Mia, and I'm going to have you again, once wasn't enough." I crash my lips against hers again, and she melts against me.

Yes, she's mine and her body knows it, now it's time to get her head to catch up.

TEN

Mia

How does he do it? One kiss and I'm putty in his hands. I still don't think this is right, but when I'm around him, I feel safe, I feel loved, and I feel sexy. It's weird, I don't feel this way around anyone else, and Hudson screams bad boy. I know Lacey believes he's dangerous, and I agree to a certain extent, but I can't see him being a drug dealer, hell I can't see him killing someone. Surely if he were, my mom wouldn't want me to get to know him, she'd be doing everything in her power to keep us away from one another.

I stare up at him, wanting more of him, wishing he'd push me against the wall and fuck me. I know that it's wrong, our parents are married. I shouldn't even be having these thoughts. His hands go to my ass, and he gently squeezes my cheeks. "Hudson, God, why are you doing this to me?" I whisper, willing myself to walk away but I'm rooted to the spot, he has that pull on me that my body and heart are drawn to him.

"Because Mia, you're mine. You walked into my club and totally eclipsed everyone. Your beauty outshone everyone there, but the best thing about you is that smile of yours. Once you came home with me you cemented the fact that you were mine." His amber eyes darken as his hands tighten on my ass.

"But we don't even know each other." I remind him. Hell, I know nothing about him besides his name and that he owns Synergy.

He pulls me against him and I can feel his erection. I bite back my moan. "Princess, we have all the time in the world to get to know each other."

I shake my head. He seems to have an answer for everything. "You're a smooth talker Hudson Brady."

His smirk is annoying but sexy, "You want a date?"

I narrow my eyes at him, "Have you ever dated anyone?"

His eyes widen as he shakes his head. "No, I don't date." He says it as if it's the most ludicrous thing in the world.

"That's a shame." I don't know why but I feel like someone's punched me in the gut, I shouldn't be surprised that he doesn't date, but I feel a sense of loss that we won't be. Not that we could ever, not now that we're siblings.

"Mia, I'm not an ordinary man, I'm not like those boys you're used to." His hand reaches up, and he brushes a stray hair that's coming down across my cheek to behind my ear. "I've done some fucked up things Mia, that's just who I am."

Looking up into those deep amber eyes of his, "I'm not used to anything Hudson." I confess, "All I know is what you taught me."

His eyes close almost as if he's in pain. "Princess, fuck," he growls, his hand resting on my cheek.

"Hudson, why do I want you when I know I shouldn't?" The words are out of my mouth before I even think, I shouldn't have said them, he's already making this hard for me to walk away and now I've just handed him the ammunition to ramp it up even more.

His hand goes back to my ass and his erection is

so big and thick against my stomach. "You want me because I'm yours just as you are mine. Mia, I don't give a fuck if our parents are married, as soon as I sank my dick into you almost two years ago, I knew you were it for me. To wake up and find you gone…" He shakes his head as his eyes darken. "I'm not waiting any longer." His lips descend on mine and every thought I had about walking away vanishes.

Everything he said is right. I've wanted him every day since that fantastic night we shared. He's been on my mind constantly, and as soon as I saw him again, I was drawn to him. I can't help the way I feel, the way *we* feel, and we're not technically doing anything wrong.

I wrap my hands around his neck as our kiss deepens. I need him, God, I need him so much. "Hudson," I breathe as I tear my mouth away from his. "I want you." My eyes pleading with him, as my hands move down to his shirt buttons.

He smiles, his hands tighten on my ass cheeks, and the next thing I know I'm being lifted into the air, I quickly wrap my arms around his neck, holding onto him for dear life. "About fucking time. I've been hard all night from just staring at you.

Mia, when I take you, it's going to be hard and it's going to be fucking fast. I'll make it up to you later."

I whimper at his words, "Hurry." I beg him, and he wastes no time, he walks with me in his arms towards his bedroom, my feet dangling in mid-air as the dress I'm wearing is tight and I can't wrap them around his waist. I don't pay attention to his room, I'm in a lust-filled haze, one that's like tunnel vision, all I see is him.

He gently lowers me until my feet hit the ground, his fingers go to my dress and he slowly begins to unzip it. I swear he's doing it antagonizingly slow just to mess with me. My dress falls to the floor, the material pooling at my feet. Taking my hand, he steadies me as I step out of it, "Perfection," he says as his eyes rake over my body, darkening as he gets to my lacy thong. "Shit." He curses as he roughly pulls off his suit jacket and kicks off his shoes.

I stand here shyly looking at him, God, I feel so stupid. Why am I so nervous? It's not as though we've not done this before.

His fingers go to the button of his pants, and his cell rings. I watch as the lust leaves his face as the phone continues to ring. When he reaches into the pocket of his pants, it's like a bucket of cold water has been thrown over me.

"Yeah?" He answers the phone, and everything hits me at once. This is my step-brother. We shouldn't be doing this. God, if Mom finds out she'll go crazy. I reach for my dress and quickly pull it on as Hudson talks to whoever he's on the call with. "Want to tell me why you waited until now to call?"

I manage to zip my dress up, and I don't say anything to him as I leave his room, I doubt he's even noticed that I've gone. Looking at the floor, I close the door behind me and on us. There's no way we would work, no matter how much Hudson believes that I'm his and vice versa, it wouldn't work. Everyone knows that our parents are married; being together is not right, of that I'm sure.

"Oh, there you are." Mom's voice makes me look up and I see her standing outside my room. She frowns, "What were you doing in Hudson's room?"

My breath leaves me in a whoosh, and guilt eats away at me. This is why we shouldn't be doing what we were just about to do. Everyone will disapprove and not only that, it's weird, our parents are married.

"Nothing." I lie, "He was trying to find out who it was that was on the door the night I went to the club." The door behind me opens, and instantly I feel that pull, "But he wouldn't listen. It was almost two years ago now, what happened that night happened a long time ago, it's time to move on and make sure it never happens again."

Mom looks at me and then behind me. I don't turn, I know if I do my resolve will wane, and I'll be in his arms. "I'm upset that you lied to me Mia, I wanted to check on you, I know that you get upset whenever you talk about your dad."

A lump forms in my throat and I blink back the tears. I don't want to talk about this, not here, not now. "I'm fine." I lie once again, "I'm just tired Mom." I whisper as I walk toward her.

She opens her arms out wide, and I willingly walk into them, "Love you, Mia."

"Love you too Mom," I reply as I wrap my arms around her waist and squeeze tight.

"We'll talk tomorrow." Mom whispers and I know what she means, tomorrow we're going to have an open and honest discussion about everything and anything. She'll ask me questions and expect honesty, and I don't think I can do that about Hudson and I. Although she has no reason to suspect anything as long as I manage to keep my distance.

"Okay Mom, is everyone gone?" I ask as I pull away from her, that magnetic feeling I have is still strong, which means that Hudson is still standing there.

She reaches for my hair and pushes it behind my ear, "Yes, they're all gone, and Harrison and I are going to turn in. I just wanted to check on you first."

I smile, "I'm pleased for you, Mom. You and Harrison seem really happy." I shrug, "That's all that I could ask for after Dad died."

"He'd be so proud of you, Mia, just as I am." She presses a soft kiss on my cheek, "Sweet dreams."

I give her a soft smile as I walk to my door, placing a hand on the handle I turn and see her, she's walking toward the stairs. Hudson, however, is standing against the wall with his arms crossed over his chest. "Night Mom. See you in the morning." I call out.

"Goodnight Mia, goodnight Hudson." She tells us as she starts to descend the stairs.

"You left, *again*." His eyes flashing as he stalks toward me. "Why?"

I press down on my door handle and push it open. "You were busy, and I'm tired. Goodnight Hudson." I turn and before I can walk one step his hand clamps around my arm. I sigh, "Hudson please don't do this." I beg. I know that I'm not strong enough to say no to him.

"Mia, look at me." He demands and instantly my eyes shoot up to his. "What's going on?"

"Hudson, we shouldn't be doing this." My hand reaches out for his. I swallow trying to make my mouth less dry. "I feel like a broken record. I want you, God, I want you so badly. But at the same time, I feel so much guilt, like what we're doing or going to do is wrong. Dirty even." I confess.

He smirks, "I like dirty."

I shake my head, "I'm being serious, and you think it's a joke."

His hand goes to my head and pulls me towards him, "No, we're two consenting adults, and we can damn well do as we please. Mia, if you don't want me, say the word and I'll walk out of this room now."

I can't say that. I can't tell him I don't want him. I do, I want him more than I've ever wanted anything in my life.

"Mia, I hate games. I get that you're conflicted,

but this shit has to stop. I don't give a fuck who knows that we're together. You need to sort your head out."

I feel bad. My head's all over the place. I have no idea what to do about this: the thought of telling everyone we're together makes my stomach flip. But the thought of not being with Hudson makes my heart hurt.

"Don't answer, just think," he says as he releases me and turns away. My heart sinks, he's walking away. Even though my brain is relieved, it'll give me a chance to think about what's going to happen.

I get changed into my pajamas. They're a cute peach lacy short set Mom got me for Christmas. They're my favorite as they're comfortable and Lacey tells me I look hot while wearing them. Climbing into bed, I shut off the light, my entire body is aching and my eyelids are heavy. I close my eyes and sink further into the pillow, ready to fall into a deep sleep.

My door opens, and I'm sitting up instantly, my hand reaching over and hitting the lamp to switch it on. "What?" I ask as I blink, my eyes adjusting to the light.

"Shhh," the bed dips beside me. "Shut the light

off." Hudson's deep voice instructs as he climbs in beside me.

I do as he asks and settle back into bed, "Good night, Hudson."

His arm goes around my stomach, and he places a kiss on my head. "Night Mia." He whispers. I turn so that we're facing each other, his hot breath against my face. "Close your eyes."

I smile, "Thanks for sleeping with me." I think it's really sweet that he came here tonight.

"Woman, you're not sleeping." He growls, and I lay my head against his shoulder and close my eyes.

Within minutes I'm fast asleep.

"Ummm." I moan, my eyes fluttering open. I'm extremely aroused, and when I finally wake I realize why. "Hudson." I moan again as his finger sinks into my pussy. My hands dive into his hair as he begins to finger fuck me.

"Like that?" He questions and I pout when he removes his finger. "You're going to love this." He assures me, a smirk on his face and those gorgeous amber eyes so dark with lust. He pulls down my pajama shorts, and it takes all I have not to turn and hide my nakedness from him.

His finger goes back inside me and I whimper, needing more. My body takes over and I grind against him. His other hand begins to trail up my stomach, under my top and toward my breast. Within seconds he's teasing my erect nipple. I bite my lip to stop the moan from escaping as I continue to grind against his finger.

"That's it, Princess, fuck my finger." His voice, deep and gravelly.

Shit, why is that so fucking hot? I want him to talk to me like that all the time, I'd be wet constantly.

"Hudson," I beg as he adds another finger inside of me, my back arches off the bed, my eyes closing as the pleasure overtakes me. The bed dips beneath me as I feel his weight on me. "Shit." I curse as his hot wet mouth clamps around my nipple. His fingers withdraw from my pussy and I whimper at the loss. His teeth pull on my nipple, and I'm so close, I can feel the warmth building. "Hudson, I want you to be inside me," I beg him.

He lets my nipple go with a pop, and looks me in the eye, "You want me, Princess?"

I nod, needing him. His eyes light up, "As you

wish." He lifts off me and anticipation builds, as I realize he's only in his boxer shorts. Where did his clothes go? Did he come to bed like that last night?

"GOD!" I cry out as his tongue laps at my clit.

"Not God." He chuckles around my clit, sending vibrations through my body.

"Hudson, please. Oh God, please." I beg. I'm so freaking close. I need to come.

His teeth gently nip at my clit, and I detonate, colored spots blur my vision, but before I'm even able to recover, Hudson thrusts into me. I cry out. He's so big, it hurts.

"Shh, Princess, give it a second and the pain will ease." His voice is gentle, something that I never thought he'd be.

I nod, I'm unable to speak, but he's right, the pain is slowly fading. "I'm sorry," I whisper.

His jaw clenches, and he shakes his head, "Don't apologize, I want to fuck you so bad, but you're sore, so I'm going to take it slow."

Now it's my turn to shake my head, "No, I'm okay now. Hudson, give it to me." I want him, all of him. I don't want him to hold back. He has a furrow in his brow. He's conflicted. "Give it to me," I demand.

His hand sneaks around the back of my neck,

and he pulls my head toward him. His lips capturing mine and he begins to move, slowly. Ever so fucking slowly.

He tears his mouth away from me, both of us breathing hard. "You sure you want this?"

Is he for real? "How many times do I have to ask?"

A quick nod of his head, he begins to move. Thrusting in and out of me, hard and fast.

"Yes." I cry out, this is what I want, him totally losing control.

His hands grip my legs, and he lifts them, putting them up against his chest, and up around his neck. He pounds into me like a man possessed. It feels as though he's hitting the opening to my cervix. Each and every time he thrusts into me I whimper, my body climbing higher again, it's not going to take much longer for me to come apart again.

A sheen of sweat lines Hudson's forehead, his breathing ragged as his hands grip my legs tighter, I'd be surprised if I wasn't bruised later on.

He closes his eyes as he thrusts inside of me once more, I gasp when I feel the warmth of his cum inside of me. "Hudson, you're not wearing a condom." Panic starts to rise within me, how could we be so careless?

He pulls out of me and lies down beside me, pulling me into his arms. "I didn't think Princess, whatever happens, it's going to be okay. There's no point in worrying about it now." He pulls the covers up over us.

"Why do you call me Princess?" I ask as I lay my head against his chest; the sound of his heart beating is soothing.

"Someday soon, I'll explain everything to you." He murmurs as he kisses my head.

"That sounds ominous." I'm intrigued about why he calls me it. As for him explaining everything else to me, I don't want to know. I don't think I ever want to know. There's an air of danger around him, the way the men call him boss, with so much respect. It makes me wonder who he really is, and my mind runs immediately to everything that Lacey has told me. No matter how hard I try and not believe it, something is niggling at me, making me think that maybe there's more truth to it than I think. We lay here in silence, and it's not long before I'm falling to sleep, the soft snores tell me that Hudson's already asleep. I'm still lying on his chest, his arm around me, and I want to stay here, I feel secure here, loved, cherished. It's not something I'm used to but something I could definitely get accustomed to.

A knock on the door has my entire body freezing. I send a silent prayer that Hudson locked the door when he came in last night. "Mia? You in there?" Shit it's my mom. The handle of the door goes down, and I brace myself. "Mia?" She calls unable to open the door.

"Yeah, Mom?" I call out making my voice deeper than it usually is.

"I woke you, I'm sorry. I thought I heard you were awake. It must have been Hudson, he's not in his room. Go back to sleep, it's still early." She tells me, and relief hits me.

"Okay Mom, see you in a while."

I hear her footsteps as she begins to descend the stairs, of course, Hudson begins to chuckle. "That was close," I tell him, relieved that he locked the door last night.

He looms over me, his dick hard against my stomach, "You need to relax Princess."

I sigh, he's right, I do. "Okay," I tell him as I relax into my pillow my hand reaching for his dick.

"You made your choice?"

I don't speak. Instead, I let my actions speak for

me. I wrap my hand around his dick and give him a squeeze.

His eyes flash, "Good girl." He murmurs and his lips descend on mine, my hand around his dick beginning to move up and down, making him pulse in my hand as I do so.

ELEVEN

Mia

Hudson left while I was having a shower. That was a close call this morning, and it's not the way I'd want my mom to find out what's happening between Hudson and I. Yet, I have no idea what's going to happen. What do we do when I go back to Phoenix? My mind's whirling with doubts, but whenever I look at him, those doubts fade and hope surfaces. There's something about Hudson that makes me feel grounded. Like he's going to be here for me no matter what. We've been sneaking around for two days now, it's exciting and new, but I know that it won't be long before it comes out. That's something that I'm not looking forward to.

"Hey Lacey, you okay?" I ask as I step into her

room, she's been withdrawn today and I'm wondering what's up with her.

"I got a phone call this morning. My parents are on their way home. My grandmother's taken a turn for the worst." Her voice shaky as she looks down at her phone.

"When are you going?" As much as I want her to stay with me for the summer, family comes first, and this could be the last time she sees her grandmother.

"Tomorrow morning." Tears shine in her eyes.

Walking over to the bed, I sit down beside her, "It'll be okay." I whisper as I reach for her hand. It's a lie. It's never okay. It hurts like hell to lose someone you love and especially someone you're close to like she is with her grandmother and I was with my dad.

"Can we do something today? Get my mind off going home?"

I nod instantly, "Yes, Mom wants to have a chat first." I roll my eyes dreading whatever it is she wants to talk about. "As soon as we're finished, we'll go out. Anywhere you want to go?"

She shrugs, her skin paler than I've ever seen it before.

"Okay, maybe we'll go to the movies or

something. Let me get this chat out of the way first, then we can drive until we decide. How does that sound?" I feel useless just sitting here unable to help the pain that is no doubt about to hit her, I wish I could wrap her up in cotton wool but I can't.

"That sounds good, thanks, Mia."

I wink at her as I stand from the bed, "Anytime. I'll see you in a bit." I tell her, as I walk out of her room.

"Mom?" I call out as I descend the stairs, this house is huge, it's a wonder I've not got lost in it already.

"In here, Mia." She yells, and I follow the sound of her voice to the sitting room.

"Is everyone gone?" I ask as I enter the room, to find her sitting alone, the TV not even on.

"Yeah, it's just us girls here at the moment." She pats the sofa beside her for me to sit down.

Taking a seat, I tell her about Lacey. "Lacey's going home tomorrow. Her grandmother's taken a bad turn."

"Oh no, does Lacey need anything? Does she need us to book her flights? Or does she have them booked? Are her parents on their way back?" She fires off question after question.

"Whoa, Mom." I say, "I don't really know much

about what's going on. Lacey has just told me what's happened and that she'll be going home."

Mom reaches for her phone and fires off a text, "Okay, I'll have Harrison sort everything out. He'll find out if she's booked on a flight or not."

"Do I even want to know how he would know that?" I watch her expression shutter. "I'll take that as a no." So much for an honest conversation. "So what did you want to talk about?"

"I'm worried about you, Mia, you've been distant." She reaches for my hand and places both hands over it. "Ever since you found out that I was married, you haven't really been yourself."

Shit, I didn't think she noticed. "I'm hurt Mom. You didn't tell me that you were seriously dating anyone, the next thing I know is you're married. I thought that you didn't want me there." I'm proud that I managed to keep my voice even and keep calm. I don't want us to argue. She's the only family that I have.

"Oh, Mia." She cries, "I never wanted you to feel that way."

"Mom, if it were the other way around, how would you feel?"

A sigh escapes her, "I'm sorry baby, I never meant to hurt you."

"You're happy that's the main thing. I like Harrison, Mom. He's good for you." From what I've seen, he worships the ground she walks on.

"He is, I don't think I've ever been this happy."

Pain hits me, "What about Dad?"

"Mia, your father and I were happy. But we both knew that we weren't meant to be together."

I swallow harshly a few times trying to find the right words to say. "What do you mean you weren't meant to be together? Mom, you and Dad were married for fifteen years."

She nods, "I know baby, we fell in love when we were young. By the time we graduated high school, we were planning on going our separate ways, he wanted to go into the army, and I wanted to travel the world."

I frown, "So what happened?"

"You happened!" She says simply, "I found out I was pregnant and your dad and I decided that we'd raise you together."

"You didn't love Dad?" I'm trying to wrap my head around this, but it feels as though everything I believed has been a lie.

"Yes and no. I loved your father, I really did. But not in the way a woman should love her husband."

"So why get married?"

"Things weren't how they are now. Being a single mom was frowned upon." She looks at me as though I should know this. “I honestly didn’t have the courage to go against your grandparents, it was hard. I had four adults telling me that I had to marry your father. Your father wanted to marry me too, he believed it was best for everyone involved if we did.” She shakes her head furiously, almost if she’s trying to get a memory out of her mind. Suddenly a smile forms on her face. “Your dad, he was so happy that we were pregnant, he couldn’t wait to be a dad.”

I smile, “He was the best dad.”

“That he was, he would talk to my bump every day. He’d tell you all about his day as we got into bed, once he was finished, he’d kiss the bump.”

I laugh, “He did that up until he died. He’d always tell me about his day, and every night before bed, he’d kiss the top of my head.” I took it for granted. I miss those moments so much. I wish I could have one more kiss on the head.

“He was a good man, he deserved better than the marriage we had.” She tells me softly, her eyes swimming with tears.

“Where would you have gone traveling?” It’s one thing I never knew Mom wanted to do.

"Asia, it's someplace I've always wanted to go. I'd love to see the culture firsthand. If I had the time or the money, I would have gone to Europe after. Ideally, I would have loved to travel the world. Meet new people and see new things but it was never meant to be. Instead, I got pregnant and married your father." She doesn't sound sad about it, just resigned.

Maybe Harrison can take her traveling, she seems really happy with him, and that could be something they do together and create lasting memories? "Do you regret it?"

She doesn't even think about her answer, she opens her mouth and the words spew out. "Yes, I had so many plans. I wanted to see the world and have fun. It was something I had dreamed of for so long, but I couldn't do that while I was pregnant nor while you were growing up. Not only that, I was married to a man I didn't love for a long time. Everything I wanted vanished in the blink of an eye."

My breath catches, and I try everything in my power to try and breathe normally. The pain of her words hits me hard. Wow. just wow. I stand up, "I didn't mean did you regret having me, Mom. Geez, eant did you regret marrying Dad. But at least I know where I stand now."

"Mia, I didn't mean it like that."

I shake my head, "Whatever, I'm going out. I'll see you later."

Stepping out of the living room, Lacey's standing there with such sadness in her eyes. "How much did you hear?" I ask her.

Her cheeks flame as she ducks her head. "I'm sorry."

"Don't be. Are you okay?"

She scoffs, "You're seriously asking if I'm okay? Mia, I just heard what your mom said to you, are you okay?"

No, I'm not okay, but what can I do about it? "I'm okay, shall we go?" I need to get out of here, I really want to see Hudson, to have his arms wrap around me and just hold me, but I don't have his number, so I have no way of getting in contact with him.

She gives me a weird look but doesn't comment. Instead, she nods.

"Okay, let me run and grab my purse. If you're ready, you can meet me in the car?" I tell her as I place my hand on the banister of the stairs.

She links her arm through mine, "I need to get

my cell phone. My mom told me she'll let me know if there's any news."

Lacey and I sit in front of the laptop, making sure that both of us are able to be seen. "What's wrong, Mia?" Sarah asks as soon as she answers, her eyes narrowing as she looks between Lacey and I. She looks good today, less stressed.

Lacey and I drove around for hours, we went for lunch and drove around for a while longer, neither of us in a hurry to come back here, as soon as we did, we rushed upstairs and called Sarah. I'm doing everything in my power to keep away from Mom. I'm still hurting over her words, I understand that she didn't mean it to come out quite the way it did, but the sentiment was there. That's what hurts.

"Hey, I wanted to find out what happened with you and Jagger? So spill, I've been on tenterhooks all day waiting to call you." I smile, mad at myself for making her worry, she has enough stress as it is.

Her eyes light up, "He emailed me last night, I was so shocked. He told me that my email was the first time he knew of me being pregnant."

Ve know that, so what happened?" Lacey's impatience shining through.

Sarah laughs, "Yeah, so I found him on Facebook and Facetimed him. I needed to see his face when he told me. I believe him, do you?" She's so unsure of herself.

"Yeah, I believe him. Sarah, there's no way he's lying." I tell her honestly, as I remember his face when I told him about Allie.

Relief shines brightly in her eyes. "He's already called today, twice. Allie smiled when she heard his voice. It was the strangest thing but also the cutest."

I'm so happy for them. It's all she's ever wanted, for Allie to know her dad. "Is he coming to see you both?"

Her face falls, and I immediately feel like an ass. "Not yet, he told me that he wishes he could but right now, with things happening he can't. But he's hoping he'll be out here soon."

"What about you two? Are you going to go there?" Lacey asks the question I've been dying to find out.

"I don't know, when we spoke yesterday, it was all about Allie. I'm not sure if I would go there again. I was burned before." She gives us a small smile. "What about you, Mia? What's happened with you and Hudson? Did you talk?"

Heat rises in my cheeks, shit, I should have known that she'd ask. I was surprised that Lacey hadn't asked me.

"Oh, wow, that good, huh?" Sarah laughs.

"We kind of picked up where we left off." I bite my lip as I wait for their responses.

"Nice!" Sarah hoots. "Was it as good as you remember?"

I can't help the grin that forms on my face, "Better." I confess, "But guys, I feel so guilty, like what we're doing is wrong."

Sarah's nose crinkles, "Why is it wrong?"

"They're brother and sister." Lacey explains, "It would be weird for some people."

My heart sinks, I didn't think she'd think that way. God, now I'm re-thinking everything I thought I had sorted out.

"Mia, I don't think that." She reaches out and touches my hand. "I promise you, I don't. I watched you and Hudson last night. You two are made for each other. It's clear to see that you both really care about each other, even though you had only spent one night with each other."

Mia, do you like Hudson?" Sarah asks, her voice tight as she does so.

"Yes, I really do."

She nods, "Then fuck what everyone else thinks. You and Hudson do what you guys need to do to be happy."

I laugh, "So ladylike."

She gives me the middle finger salute.

"She's right Mia, you need to do what makes you happy. If anyone has a problem, it's their problem. But if people see you two together, they'll understand." Lacey tells me, and I smile, my girls are amazing, they have my back no matter what.

"Any other gossip?" Sarah asks, and I laugh. She's lonely and lives vicariously through us, although we don't have much to tell, usually.

"Well..." I begin, "I want to know what happened between Barney and Lacey last night." I smirk as Lacey glares at me. So something *did* happen.

"Oh my!" Sarah gasps as Lacey ducks her head, "Miss Lacey, spill."

When she finally lifts her head, her face is as red as a tomato, "We kissed. Well, he kissed me."

I roll my eyes, "Did you like it?"

Sarah laughs, "Look at her face, of course she

did!"

"Lace?" I ask, trying not to laugh as she hides her face behind her hands.

"Yes." It's a squeak, but we hear it.

"Tell us everything," Sarah begs.

I'm so happy for Lace. She needs someone in her life who will make her blush like she is now.

"I went to bed, and he followed me up not long afterward. He knocked on my door and I had just put on my pajamas." She shakes her head, a small smile on her lips, "His hand reached to the back of my neck, and he pulled me toward him."

"Holy shit!" Sarah whispers, "That is freaking hot."

"She's not wrong. What happened after that?" I ask, wondering where it went.

"I don't know how long the kiss lasted, but he pulled away and said goodnight. He walked away without saying another word. I have no idea what is going on. I mean, did he kiss me for the hell of it? I'm confused."

Oh, poor Lace. "Well then while he's here, ignore the ass until he says something," I tell her, I'd be pissed too if Hudson did that to me. I respect that he doesn't like playing games. Everything's out in the open with him.

"Mia's right. Don't let him treat you like that. Ignore the jerk. No doubt he's waiting for you to say something to him first. No, let the ass see what it's like to be ignored." Sarah's eyes are narrowed, if she were here, she'd kick Barney's ass.

Lacey sighs, "Yeah, it's just..." She trails off, as if she's scared to say it.

"Just what?" I ask as I reach for her hand, this time I'm offering her support,

"It's just that it was amazing. I've never felt that way when I've been kissed before. I got butterflies in the pit of my stomach."

"Yep, I know what those feel like." I give her a reassuring smile. She's not alone here. Men are hard to understand and us girls need to stick together.

"When I see him, I just want to be around him. Does that make sense?" She's so unsure, and I hate that she's feeling this way.

"It makes total sense. Trust me, Lace, we've all been there." Sarah tells her and Allie's cries pierce my eardrums. "I've got to go, I'll catch up with you both tomorrow."

"Bye." I wave, and she ends the call. Turning to Lace, "You never told her about your grandmother."

She shrugs, "And you never told her about what happened with your mom."

I shake my head, "She doesn't need to hear about that. She's got enough going on."

"Yeah, do you think she'll move back to California now that Jagger wants Allie in his life?"

"I don't know. It's hard because it's what she wants. To be around Jagger for the sake of Allie but she hates Cali, if she could be anywhere else in the world she would be. Time will tell." If Jagger doesn't move, I can see her coming back, but she won't go back to Oakland. That's one place she'll never step foot in again.

Lacey's phone buzzes and she stares down at it in shock. "Um Mia, your mom and Harrison have paid for my ticket back to Carson City."

"Good. What time's your flight?"

She looks at her phone again, "Ten."

I nod, "That's plenty of time."

"For what?" She asks wearily.

"Oh, you'll see, I have plans for us tonight," I smirk, tonight is going to get both our minds off everything.

We're going to a party in Malibu. A friend of mine is living there and having a party. It'll be good to get away from here for a while.

TWELVE

Hudson

Everyone is sitting around the table having dinner, enjoying the meal. Jagger and Martin are shoveling food into their mouths like they've never been fed, both Barney and Lacey keep glaring at each other, I wonder what happened between them last night. Whereas Mia's sitting there with a satisfied smile on her face, she's like a drug, and I'm already addicted to her. Although I knew she was something special the very first time we met, she's had me in a tailspin ever since then. Not that I'd ever admit that shit to anyone. I don't need my enemies learning of the woman who means something to me. It's bad enough that they may accidentally stumble across her because our parents are married. I can just see those fuckers salivating at the prospect of getting to my woman.

My enemies saw me when I was a punk-ass kid, they don't know me now; they have no idea that I'd kill them with my bare hands without so much as a second thought. Not only am I a mean sonofabitch, I have a lot of friends in a lot of high places. Not only do I have the mayor of California in my pocket, I also have members of the police departments on my payroll. So far I have at least three from each department here in California, not to mention the commissioner himself is my godfather. That is a fucking laugh right there. He and my father were best friends when growing up, the commissioner's father was my grandfather's right-hand man, we've all grown up together, it was expected that the commissioner's son Travis would join the ranks and be a soldier, maybe even work his way up but I wouldn't allow it. His old man's a cop. There's no way in hell that I'd let him in.

I know a lot of organized crime leaders, too many to have someone so close to a cop know the ins and outs of my operation, to know who is in my inner circle or outer circle so to speak as I don't trust many people. Those that I do are the ones closest. Jagger and Martin, they're the only ones that I trust, although I wouldn't say implicitly. I've known many a man to betray those closest and being in this business, I'm cautious.

"Son, how long are you staying here for?" Dad asks me, and I look up at him just in time to see him glance at Tina.

Ah, she doesn't like me. She seems okay, a bit of a hypocrite. She knew what my dad was when she slept with him. One was being married, the other was being the boss. She got him to give up both of those things, leaving my mom a fucking mess. Although the way hers and Dad's relationship was, it's a good thing they're apart. Mom sees that she was betrayed and is raging mad. It's why I've not been to see her in a couple of weeks, the conversation always turns to Dad, and I'm done with hearing about it.

"Don't know yet. Is there a time limit on my stay?" Even though my tone's even, and I'm smiling, I'm pissed.

"Of course not," Tina tells me, her eyes wide, I think there's a hint of terror in them.

"Son I'm not trying to get rid of you, you have your own house and a business. I was just wondering how long you were staying." Damn, he's eager to get rid of me, and I'm wondering if it's him or Tina.

Mia snorts, "So, Lacey and I have our own place, you've not asked how long we're staying."

"Mia!" Tina reprimands, but it's too late, we're all laughing.

"What?" Mia looks innocent, like she has no idea what was wrong with what she said.

"Mia, this is a conversation between Harrison and Hudson."

I watch in amusement as Mia looks around the table, "Oops, my bad. I thought it was a family discussion, you know, with it being at the dinner table and all."

Tina's eyes narrow, "Mia...." She warns, "We'll discuss this later."

"Discuss what?" Dad asks his jaw clenching as he looks between a visibly shaken Mia and a wide-eyed Tina. I too would like to know what the hell is going on.

"Watch out Harrison. Mom may regret marrying you too soon." Mia snarls, fuck, I'm going to kill whoever upset her.

"Mia!" Tina exclaims. "Stop, we'll talk about it later."

Mia rolls her eyes and stands from the table, "I

don't want to discuss it, Mom, you've said what you wanted, just leave it." Mia looks pissed.

"You took what I said the wrong way." Tina stares at her daughter in despair.

Mia shakes her head, "It's what you said Mom, there was no other way to take it." Tears are in her eyes as she walks out of the kitchen, leaving all of us wondering what the hell just happened.

Lacey throws her napkin onto the table and pushes her chair from out under the table, "I'll go." She shakes her head at Tina, fuck how do I not know what the hell happened?

"Lacey..." Tina begins, but Lacey shakes her head.

"Mrs. Brady, I respect you a lot. You're like a second mom to me, and that's why I'm not going to say anything right now." Lacey walks toward the door. Once she gets there she turns and faces us, "I have to say this…" She says, and I want to laugh, she needs to make up her mind.

“Mia's been through a lot, she's lost her dad, and she's hurt because you never told her you were dating or that you were getting married. I was surprised that she wanted to come here this summer, she wasn't planning to, especially when she found out about your marriage. But what you said to her," She shakes her head in disgust, "You hurt her more than anything." She walks out of the dining room without another word.

I want to get up and go after her, but I need to find out what the hell just happened.

"Tina, what's wrong?" I don't think I've ever heard my dad sound so... soft. "What did Mia take the wrong way?"

Tina begins to weep softly, and Dad's beside her within seconds. "Tina, it can't be that bad..."

"She hates me." She weeps, "I need to talk to her." She tells my dad as she stands and pushes past him and rushes out of the room.

Dad sighs as he turns back to the table, "Jagger, Barney, would you give us a minute?"

I sit back in my chair and cross my arms as I wait for the guys to vacate the room.

"Son..." He begins as he reaches for his bottle of beer. "What the hell are you playing at?"

My nostrils flare, "Dad...." I say through clenched teeth, "What the fuck are you talking about?"

He shakes his head. "The business is yours," he says as if that's supposed to appease me. "I'm talking about this shit you're doing with Mia. Christ, are you fucking crazy?"

I'm on my feet within seconds, "What I do is none of your business." How fucking dare he?

"It is my business." He fires back, "She's family Hudson. How could you fucking sleep with her? I heard you two last night and again this morning. Our bedroom is below Mia's. I'm not stupid either son. I saw the way you two were the night of our party. Of all the women in the world, why did you have to pick her? Hudson you could have your pick of any woman out there, leave Mia alone." His hand bangs down on the table as he shouts at me.

I place my hands down on the table and lean forward, so we're almost face to face. "I won't leave her alone. We're two consenting adults Dad. You have no say in what goes on between us."

He throws the bottle across the room, the glass shattering as it impacts against the wall. "You have to realize Hudson, that just because you want something, it doesn't mean you can have it. She's your sister."

I step back in disgust. This is exactly what Mia didn't want. "That's utter fucking bull, and you know it. Unless you're her father, then Dad, you've some explaining to do."

His feet are silent against the tiled floor as he paces the room, "Hudson, don't be an ass. I'm serious, leave Mia alone. I don't understand you've been going crazy about finding this mystery girl for what two years now and then all of a sudden you're all over Mia. Are you trying to sabotage my marriage?"

A bitter laugh escapes me, "I couldn't give two fucks about your marriage. The mystery girl *is* Mia Dad. It happened the night she came to Synergy. I won't leave her alone. We were together before you and Tina got together."

"Fuck." His jaw is grinding.

I laugh, "Tina doesn't want me near her daughter? I'm not a fucking monster." Well, not to Mia anyway.

He cuts me a side glance, "She knows what you do, Hudson, she's not real happy that you're here while Mia is."

"Wow, look at you Dad, you're a fucking peach!" I shouldn't be surprised, he's always put himself first. "How much of a hypocrite is Tina, huh? I mean she knew what you did and she still fucking slept with you. Oh, she also knew you were married, and that didn't stop her either. Yet *I'm* the bad guy."

Movement in my peripheral vision. Fuck. Mia's standing there with doe eyes, "You were married when you and Mom started dating?" She shakes her head, "I don't even know that woman anymore." She turns around, and both Dad and I follow behind her.

"Mia, why were you listening to their conversation?" Tina grabs her arm to stop her from going any further and I want to rip her arm away, Mia looks fucking gutted, and I want to hurt Tina for making her look that way.

"Son, don't. This is between them." Dad whispers to me. He's right. Mia won't thank me for getting involved.

Mia's laugh is bitter, "Oh, everything is someone else's fault. I mean, I just found out that you slept with a married man. You broke up a marriage Mom and yet I shouldn't have overheard a conversation where they were screaming at each other. What was I supposed to have done? Shoved ear-buds in my ears?"

I bite back the chuckle. Damn Mia's pissed.

"Mia, you ready?" Lacey asks coming down the stairs, and I glance at her. She's wearing a short dress and heels. Turning my attention back to Mia, I see that she too is in a short fucking dress and heels. Her ass would be shown if she bent over.

"Ready? Where are you going?" Tina asks looking between the girls.

"Yep, ready." Mia smiles, and it's the first genuine smile I've seen on her beautiful face tonight.

"Mia?" Tina asks again.

"What, Mom? Am I grounded?"

Tina's eyes roll skyward, "No, but I'd like to know where you're going."

"Out." She replies as she grabs Lacey's hand and leaves the house, slamming the door behind her as she does.

"Tina, leave her. She'll come home when she's ready. If you keep going, she's going to fight back harder."

My eyes are on the door. I need to find out where the hell she is going. The way she is tonight, she could easily end up in an accident, or worse.

"Tina, what the hell happened? You've been telling me that Mia is sweet and mild. You're upset and she's mad." Dad asks, and I turn my attention to Tina.

She sighs, "Mia and I were talking about her dad and I. I made the mistake of telling her that Rob and I weren't in love, that we were only together because I was pregnant. Because of Mia."

"Okay, but I still don't understand why Mia would be mad about that?" Dad questions, we're all getting the sense that there's more to this than just saying they didn't love each other.

"Mia said that we shouldn't have got married. I told that her back then, things were different. She asked if I regretted it… I told her I did and didn't." She glances at Dad and I just as Martin and Jagger make an appearance behind her. "I thought she meant having a baby, but she meant marrying Rob. I love Mia, she's the best thing that ever happened to me. I don't regret having her. She took what I said in the wrong context." She begins to cry, and Dad pulls her into his arms, probably to get her out of my way, she told her daughter she wished she never had her, no wonder Mia's pissed.

Jagger coughs, "Boss?"

I give Dad a glance, he's got a gripping hold of Tina and consoling her. Fucking sap. I walk over to Martin and Jagger, "What?" I ask wondering what the hell is happening now. We've yet to talk about the shit that was revealed last night. I wanted to give him time to contact Sarah and get all the facts before we start killing that fucking bitch Carina.

Martin stands a little taller, "Boss, Arturo was deported this morning, and Juan is digging to see what the hell happened. Jimmy called, Juan has a friend in immigration, he's trying to find out who reported him."

I narrow my eyes, "He won't be able to, right?"

Martin looks at me like I'm stupid. "No, he won't, it was an anonymous tip. He can look until he's blue in the face, he's never going to find out it was us."

"Okay, and you're telling me because?"

"Because, he's been calling the office looking for you." Jagger smiles at me, "The fucker is wanting your help to find out what happened to his cousin."

Of course he does, "I'll call the asshole, will you two find out where Mia and Lacey are?" I walk away and head upstairs knowing that they'll do as I ask. By the time I've finished talking to Juan, they'll have her location.

"Juan, you've been calling. Have I missed a meeting?" I don't schedule meetings with that fuck. He's a try hard, and I seriously wonder how the hell he became head of a cartel. The man shouldn't be left alone with a fucking plant, let alone an entire fucking cartel.

"Hey, Hudson, my man." My teeth grind at his words. "I've been calling because I need a favor."

His words are hard to understand as he has a very thick accent.

"What do you need?" I can't help but smile, he's an amateur and asking me for a favor proves that.

"My cousin Arturo has been deported. I want to know who informed the authorities that he was here. Then I want them taken care of."

I smile, this could be a great way to get rid of one of my enemies *and* have Juan owe me one. "This is going to cost you."

He doesn't even hesitate, "I don't care. I want this done."

"I won't be able to get your cousin back, but I'll find out who informed the authorities. I'll be in contact when I have information." I end the call, that will keep that fucker off my back for a few days.

I dial Jagger, and he answers immediately, "Where are they?"

"Malibu. Martin has the car ready and waiting."

"I'm on my way down." I hang up. It's time to get my girl.

“Hudson?” Tina says as I reach the front door.

“Yeah?” I ask, turning to face her, trying to keep my anger in check.

“Your dad told me about you and Mia.”

My hand tightens on the door handle, "Let me guess; I'm not good enough for your daughter? I need to stay away. Mia's a good girl, and she doesn't need to be led astray by me."

She tentatively takes a step toward me, "You're the Kingpin Hudson. The drug lord, baron, whatever you want to call it. You're the boss of a criminal empire. That's not something I want my daughter mixed up in."

"Shouldn't that be Mia's decision?"

She shakes her head once, "She's been hurt enough, I can't, I won't let her be hurt by you."

My nostrils flare as I try and tamp down my anger. Fuck, she's pushing me. "I won't hurt her. If Mia doesn't want me, then I walk away. That is the only way I'm going to walk away."

She throws her hands up in the air. "Why? What game are you playing with her?"

"I'm not playing a game." I glance at Dad as he comes and stands beside Tina.

"Then why won't you leave her alone?" She's crying now.

"Everything is about what you want, isn't it, Tina?" I say through clenched teeth.

"Hudson, don't," Dad warns me.

"You slept with a married man and ended my

parent's marriage. You didn't want Dad to be the boss, so you got him to quit. You don't want me with your daughter, and I'm taking it that it's you that doesn't want me here." The way her cheeks redden tells me that I've hit the nail on the head. "Have you thought about my dad and what he wants, or wanted? Because looking in, it seems like you're out for yourself and only you. Fuck what anyone else thinks."

"How dare you?" She bites out, "I love my daughter and I love my husband. I want the best for them."

I laugh, "The best isn't having me around them. Don't worry, I won't be back."

Dad steps forward. "No, this is your home as much as it is ours and Mia's. You'll come home. Go and get Mia and Lacey."

"Harrison!" Tina cries and looks to my dad, tears streaming down her face. I'd feel sorry for her if she wasn't so selfish.

"No, Tina, Hudson's right. You don't like my son because of his job. You haven't taken the time to speak to him. This is my house and my son is welcome anytime he wants." His tone menacing and Tina flinches.

Damn, I didn't see that coming. My dad never

stands up for me; he never has. I wonder what has changed. I don't ask, I turn and leave, let them two have it out and come to a decision. It's no skin off my nose if they don't want me here, I'll go. But I won't keep away from Mia.

"That was intense," Jagger comments as I step outside.

"You think?"

He pats me on the shoulder, "About time your old man started acting like one."

"Yep, enough about that shit, let's go to Malibu and get the girls." Getting into the car, I turn to Jag, "What's happening with Sarah?"

A big smile forms, "Hudson, I saw my daughter. Fuck she's amazing man."

I smile, I'm happy for him. "Good, so what're you going to do about the situation?"

His eye twitches, "I'm getting Sarah to move back here. I need her and Allie with me."

I nod, it's what I thought he'd do. "What about Carina?"

His eyes narrow, "Leave her to me; she crossed the wrong man."

That's enough for me, I'll leave her be. I know that Jagger is going to fix what was damaged with Sarah and also end her reign of terror over him.

I've let it slide long enough, and I can only bite my tongue for so long. She's a woman, and that's the only reason I've not put a bullet in her.

I lean back in my seat and close my eyes, wishing Martin would put his foot on the gas. I need to get to Mia. I want to make sure she's okay, and then I want to be inside her. I've been hard as fucking stone since I woke up this morning. Damn, she's addictive, but I like it.

THIRTEEN

Hudson

"Boss, Barney's with the girls now." Martin says, and I open my eyes, "He said that he and Lacey were talking and she told him where they were."

"Good." At least they're with my man. He'll make sure they're safe.

"Um, Boss..." Martin says tentatively.

"Martin?" I ask, getting frustrated. He knows how much I hate this fucking hesitant shit. Say what you have to and get it over and done with.

"He said Mia's not doing okay. She's sitting on the beach with Lacey, that she was crying earlier. That both the girls were."

Shit. "Did he say what upset them?"

"No, he said they were fine when he got there,

and then when Mia came out of the house she looked pissed. She and Lacey spoke and they both burst into tears."

"How long until we get there?" Now I'm on edge. She shouldn't have left the house, although I understand why she did. She's in a fragile state of mind. Fuck. Martin needs to put his foot on the gas.

"Ten minutes." He replies.

Jagger laughs, "I bet he's fucking having heart failure. That man is so tactless. He has no idea how to deal with women and their emotions."

"And this coming from Casanova himself?" I quip.

Martin chuckles, but Jag shakes his head, "You got jokes. I'm fucking amazing with women."

I give him a look. "Jag, you've had that poisonous bitch attached to your dick for almost five years now, I wouldn't exactly call that amazing with women."

He flips me off, "She went too far this time." His voice turning deadly.

"Where is she?"

"Don't worry, she's nowhere near your business," I smirk, the fucker knows me too well. "I have her in rehab at the moment. I'm not paying for it, her father is. I have enough shit on that family that I can do whatever the fuck I want, and they'll play ball." This is the Jagger that I know, the man that I made my right-hand man, not the sap that was pussy whipped because that bitch was leading him by his dick. Carina is fucked. "I'm lucky that Sarah understands that Carina is a psycho."

"Psycho? Jag, she's fucking worse than that. I'm warning you, brother. When she finds out that you're moving Sarah here with the baby, she's going to lose her shit."

He shakes his head, "I know, but Hudson, you don't know Sarah, she'll tear her head off."

I narrow my eyes, "Just how well do you know Sarah?"

He shrugs, "Her brother Frankie and I were at high school together. She was always hot, but strictly off-limits."

It's in this moment that I know why Mia never told me who let her into the club. It was Jagger. Fuck. "Jag... " My voice hard. "You willingly let two underage girls into my club?"

"Fuck you, man." He fires back, "No, I didn't. I didn't know how old she was. It had been years since I saw Frankie, since I had seen Sarah. They had IDs, fucking good ones. I'm not stupid."

"So you knew who she was, why didn't you find

her?" I have been searching for Mia since that day. I had Martin look for her, and he came up short. If I had known that Jag knew her friend, I would have had her in my bed a hell of a lot sooner.

He rolls his eyes at me, "Look, Boss, do you think I've been sitting on my ass? I knew that you slept with Mia, although I didn't know her name either. I knew that you wanted her just as I wanted Sarah. I went to Sarah's place every month, and each time I did her mom told me she'd not seen her since Sarah left. I don't think her and her mom get along."

"What about her brother?"

He shakes his head, "He's in the military Boss. He's a SEAL. He's deployed, the last time Sarah saw him, she was eight months pregnant and hid it from him. She didn't want him to worry while he was deployed."

"You need to get her home soon, by the sounds of things she's alone in New York, it's got to be hard for her Jag, not to mention lonely."

He smiles widely, "I'm working on it. Don't you worry."

I nod, that's good, if he can get Sarah home, it may help me persuade Mia to stay here in Cali too. Fucking Arizona is like a ten-hour drive, and I'm not moving there. "Have you told your mom about Allie?"

"Yep, she's dying to meet her, and I'm trying my hardest to get her to calm the fuck down and wait until Sarah's ready. But you know my ma, Hudson, she doesn't exactly know how to be patient."

"How much have you told her?"

He glances out the window before turning back to face me. "Enough, I've told her not to tell anyone else as of yet. Just wait until Ma finds out what Carina did, she'll want to be the one to kill her."

I smirk, "The fact that Mary hates Carina should have rang alarm bells for you. Mary thinks everyone is a sweetheart, she never has a bad word to say about anyone, except Carina."

He sighs, "I know, it's a clusterfuck."

"Say the word, and I'll sort it out. It'll give you more time to focus on Sarah and Allie."

"I'll think about it. Right now, she's doing a twenty-one-day stint in rehab, that gives me plenty of time to get Sarah and Allie settled at home with me and then get rid of her." He sounds like a man with a plan, and I hope it works out for him, even the best-laid plans have a way of going awry.

"Boss we're here," Martin tells me, and I immediately get out of the car. "Want us to wait?"

Just as I go to answer, Lacey and Barney walk over to us, "You two going?" I ask frowning at the black tear stains on Lacey's face.

"Yeah." He whispers, his arm around Lacey's shoulders.

"Jag, you and Martin go on without me," I tell them. Martin nods and begins to drive off.

"Mia's on the beach," Barney tells me, his arm around Lacey's back, she's stuck to his side.

"Hudson, she's okay," Lacey tells me and reaches out for my hand.

"Are you okay?" I ask as she squeezes my hand.

She shakes her head, tears swimming in her blue eyes. "My grandmother passed away."

I pull her into my arms, she wraps hers around my waist and rests her head on my chest. "I'm sorry for your loss," I tell her quietly, glancing at Barney who has a shocked expression on his face. He really needs to get a poker face, the ass. He's probably never seen me be polite to someone before.

"Thank you." She replies as I let her go. "Look after her Hudson, she's probably at the lowest she's ever been right now."

"Don't worry about Mia. I've got her." She gives me a sharp nod and climbs into Barney's car. "I'll talk to you all later on."

I walk away and toward the beach. I instantly see her as I step onto the sand, her profile lit up by the brightness of the moon. Her raven hair is blowing in the breeze, and the closer I get, the more I can see. Her heels are off, and to her side, her feet are digging into the sand. Her arms are around her legs hugging them close to her body. Her chin resting on top of her knees, her gaze focused on the beach in front of her. Lacey said she was at her lowest, to me she looks absolutely shattered. My woman looks broken and I need to fix it. No matter how broken she looks, she's still the most beautiful woman I've ever laid eyes on, and I'm a lucky fucker to know that she's mine.

I sit down beside her, not saying a word. A lone tear falls from her eye and down her cheek, she just sits there and stares out onto the beach. I leave her be, just sitting here waiting for her to talk. I know she will when she's ready. My arm reaches around her back, and I hold her. Within seconds, she's leaning against me, still not saying a word.

"Is Lacey gone?" She asks, twenty minutes later.

"Yeah, she's with Barney. He'll make sure she gets home okay." A shiver runs down her body, "Are you cold?"

She blushes as she ducks her head into my

chest, "No." She murmurs, her words low as she's talking into my chest. "Whenever you talk, I always get shivers."

I smile at her admission, "Are you ready to go back?"

She shakes her head. "I don't want to see her just yet."

I pick her up and put her on my lap, "Talk to me." I ask her as I wrap my arms around her.

Her head rests on my shoulder, and she places a kiss on my chin, "I'm probably being stupid."

I rub my hand up and down her arm. Goosebumps form and I love the reaction she has to me. "Let me be the judge of that, what happened?" I already know, but from what Tina told us, I want to hear it from Mia.

"Mom and I, we have these really honest discussions I honestly thought that she wanted to talk about us, I had it in my head that she knew about us."

"She does, Dad heard us last night." Her gasp makes me smile, "He told your mom, and she's not happy about it."

"Is your dad?" She questions, lifting her head off my shoulder. Her eyes wide and fearful. This is what she didn't want to happen.

"At first he was, then I spoke to him, you overheard that conversation."

Her cheeks flame, "I really didn't mean to." She bites her lip, "I promise I wasn't eavesdropping. You were practically screaming at one another. I never did hear you talk about us though."

I shrug, "I'm not worried that you overheard. I am sorry that you had to hear that your mom and my dad were having an affair, though." I honestly thought she knew. Everyone knew that my dad was a cheating fucking ass.

The smile she gives me is a wobbly one, her bottom lip trembling. "I don't really know who my mom is at all. Everything I'm finding out lately is shattering everything I thought I knew."

"What do you mean?"

She turns on my lap so that she's straddling me, "I grew up thinking my parents had the happiest marriage, that they were happy together. When my dad died, I hurt so bad. I was a daddy's girl. He was deployed a lot, but when he was home, they were the best times. God, I miss him terribly." She takes a deep breath, "So I went to college to escape the constant reminders that he's no longer here. I was so shocked when Mom called me to tell me she was married."

My eyes widen, "What? You didn't know they were getting married?"

She shakes her head, "No, I didn't even know they were serious. She told me she was dating, but that was it. I guess I never asked her. So when she called saying she'd gotten married, I was shocked. Fuck, I was hurt and pissed. It was as if I didn't matter. She couldn't be bothered telling her daughter that she'd met a man she liked, that she'd found love and was getting married. No, she waited until it was done before telling me."

Damn! Tina's fucking cold, she's not the woman she appears to be. I wonder if Dad knows she never told Mia?

"It felt like she was trying to run from the life she had with my dad; everything they had built together is gone. The only thing left of it is the house that she's put up for sale. The house my dad spent years paying for." Anger and sorrow fill her words, she's pissed, and right now I don't blame her. If that were me, I'd be fucking murderous.

"What happened today?"

"Ugh," she says as she shakes her head, her hair falling down around her face, I reach out and push it back behind her ear, "We sat down to talk, we got talking about Dad. She said that she didn't love

Dad. That she didn't want to marry him, the only reason she did was because her parents and my dad's wanted them to. Mom wanted to go travel the world, see the different cultures, and Dad was going into the army, just as his father had, and his grandfather. He was the seventh generation to follow in the footsteps of his forefathers."

"That's pretty commendable."

"It's all he ever knew, you know? It was what the family did. I've let them down. I didn't follow in their footsteps."

My hands frame her face, "No, Princess, you haven't." I place a kiss gently on her lips. "What else did your mom say?" I try and ask as nicely as I can even though I thoroughly dislike that woman.

"I asked her if she regretted it. I meant marrying my dad. Her response was... Yes, and no. That she had so many plans, that she wanted to see the world and have fun. It was something she had dreamed of for so long, but she couldn't do that while she was pregnant nor while I was growing up."

Yeah, Tina is a selfish bitch. Who the hell says that to her daughter?

"I know that she meant that she sometimes regrets it, or that she'd look back and wonder what if, but the culminations of the lies and secrets got to me. I can't stand the lies."

Now isn't the time to tell her what I do, but I need to, and soon, if I don't and she finds out from someone else, I could lose her.

"Do you think I'm overreacting?" She asks quietly, her gaze drifting back to the sea.

"No, I don't. I think you know how you feel and right now, you're hurt, and you have every right to be. But Mia she's your mom, you're going to have to talk to her eventually."

Her nose wrinkles in distaste. "I know. Just not now."

"Okay, time to go."

She frowns as I lift her off my lap. "Where are we going?"

Standing I pull her into my arms, "Well, you never ate dinner," I kiss her lips and she immediately melts into my body, "I can taste beer on your lips which means you've been drinking on an empty stomach." My words come out like a reprimand, but I'm not telling her off. I'm just stating the obvious.

"Okay, let's get something to eat, is there a McDonalds around here somewhere?" She asks as she reaches for her shoes.

She wants McDonalds, I'll bring her to it, I don't give a shit how far away it is. "Let's go," I tell her, and she instantly grabs my hand and holds it tightly. We walk toward her car, "You okay?" She's stopped crying and seems to be a little better, but I'm not sure if it's because she's good at hiding things deep inside.

"I suppose, I still have no idea why my mom lied nor why she hid the fact that she was getting married from me and that hurts."

I squeeze her hand, "The only way to find out is to talk to her."

She nods, "Tomorrow, I promise. Thanks, Hudson."

I pull her to a stop, and she crashes into my chest, "What are you thanking me for?"

She gets shy and glances away, "For being here."

I lift her chin so that she can look at me, "Princess, you're mine, and that means that I take care of you. I'm your man, and when you're upset I'm going to be here, so don't thank me for doing what I'm meant to do."

She reaches up on her tiptoes and kisses me, "You're a good man Hudson."

If only that were fucking true, she doesn't know the real me. I'm debating with myself if I should ever tell her. Right now though, she doesn't need to know. I'm keeping her in the dark for her own protection as well as for my own sanity. I know that if I tell her that I sell drugs and guns she's going to walk away and that cannot happen.

I take her hand again and walk to her car, "Keys." I tell her as I hold out my hand. She doesn't argue, just passes them to me. Getting in, I have to move the seat back, my six-foot-two frame doesn't fit, so I push the seat back all the way and I catch Mia smiling. "What?"

She shakes her head that smile still present, "Just thinking how good you look in my car."

I laugh, she's freaking adorable. Starting the car, it purrs to life, I put it into drive and get the hell out of here.

"Oh yeah, you definitely look good in my car." Her voice husky and her hand reaches over the gear stick and she touches my leg, her hand moving slowly upward to my dick.

Fuck, I'm hard, it's like I'm in a constant state of arousal when I'm around her. My hands grip the steering wheel tighter as she begins to unbutton my jeans. Fuck, this girl amazes me, she knows how to shock me. Her hand wraps around the base of my cock, and I hiss out a breath as she squeezes me. Christ.

My eyes are glancing around trying to find a secluded spot that I can park in and fuck her senseless. She's made my fucking year doing this. I'm harder than I've ever been and the fact that we could be seen by anyone passing by doesn't seem to affect Mia. There's a dirt road that leads toward the beach, and I take the turn just as Mia reaches over and wraps her mouth around my dick.

"Christ Mia," I say through gritted teeth, fighting the urge to pull over and thrust into her mouth until she gags.

"Mmmmmmmm." She moans around my dick and I have to grip the steering wheel tighter, my knuckles going white as I do so. Finally, fucking finally, I manage to find somewhere to park safely.

"Take your pants off," I growl, and she looks up at me as she continues to suck me. Fuck, but that is sexy as hell. I thrust into her warm mouth and hit the back of her throat, she gags and I do it again, loving the sound. Her breathing quickens, and I know it's not because she's scared or can't breathe. No, my girl is fucking turned on from me gagging her with my dick.

"Want me to come in your mouth?" I ask her, as

I thrust deep into her mouth again and she whimpers as she nods her head. Yeah, my girl is a freak, she's made for me. "Work for it," I demand, and instantly she wraps her hands around my dick again as I pulse in her hands.

I thrust into her mouth a few more times before the tingles begin at the base of my back, I'm close. "Mia, I'm going to come in your mouth," I tell her, and just as I thought, she doesn't pull away, instead she grips my dick tighter and she sucks harder. I close my eyes and lean back against the headrest and enjoy the feel of my dick inside her hot, wet mouth. Fuck, this woman is amazing.

I feel the orgasm building and I reach for her hair and thrust into her mouth... once, twice... three times before exploding.

She sits back in her seat with a smile. "I'm hungry." She comments, her eyes staring at my dick and I laugh. She shrugs and puts her seatbelt on, "What?"

I shake my head and button my jeans up, "Nothing Princess, but wait until I get you home. You're in for a shock when I fuck you senseless."

She gasps, her eyes widening before she sinks back into her seat and a cheeky smile forms, "You're sure of yourself, aren't you?"

Damn, this woman is amazing. "Oh I am, want to know why?"

"Why?" She whispers as I start the engine.

"Because your panties are soaked." Her face flames at my words, "I can smell you from here, and as soon as I get you in bed, I'm going to eat that pussy until you beg me to stop. You're going to come so hard your body is going to shake, and then, I'm going to fuck you until you're sore and raw."

She gulps, "I hope you live up to your promise."

I laugh, "On that, you have nothing to worry about. Remember that first night?" I smirk as she begins to pant. "You want food?"

She shakes her head. "I'm not hungry for food..." She leaves it hanging in the air what she is, in fact, hungry for.

I need to get her the fastest drive-thru known to man and then home and pronto.

FOURTEEN

Mia

Hudson's hand is on the base of my back, he's leading me into the house, my entire body wound up tight. The lights are on downstairs which means someone's awake and I have a feeling that it's Mom.

Hudson leans in close, his lips brushing against my ear. "Princess, it's fine, we're going to eat and then I'm taking you to bed." His gravelly voice as he murmurs in my ear sends shivers throughout my body. "How wet are you?"

I gasp and turn to face him, his arm going around me, pulling me flush against his body, his dick hard against my stomach. He seems to be in a constant state of arousal. "Hudson, when you ask questions like that, I get soaked."

He bites his lip as his eyes dilate, "Soaked?"

"Mmmhmm," I reply with a smile, being around him is so easy, and I'm actually okay at flirting with him, it's fun to tease him because his reactions are so sexy, he loves being around me. He touches me at every available opportunity. Even though he's the first guy I've been with, he makes me feel cherished, wanted, special, and most importantly loved.

Shit, is that what I'm feeling? Do I love him? I can't. It's way too soon. I mean we've only known each other two days, and I don't even know him properly. No, it's definitely not love, more like lust. Yes, caring lust. I care about him, so that's what I'm calling it.

He lifts a hand to my head, his fingers tangling in my hair, the air between us crackling with electricity. Everything around us vanishes as his lips crash down against mine, his tongue entering my mouth, this kiss is hard, dominating, and fierce, just like Hudson himself.

A coughing sound has him pulling away from me and glaring at whoever's behind me. "We'll be in, in a minute."

I turn to see who he's talking to and I'm not surprised that it's my mom. "Okay," she says softly, but there's a hardness in her eyes as she looks at the way that Hudson and I are embraced. I don't have the energy to deal with her tonight if she's going to have something to say about our relationship.

"You going to talk to her?" He asks me when Mom walks away.

I shake my head. "Not yet, maybe tomorrow. I'm not ready yet. I'm too emotional and mad at her. If we talk now, I'm going to say something I regret and things could get ugly. That's something I don't want." I love my mom, and I don't want there to be a rift between us. If I talk to her now, there very well could be.

"You shock me each and every time you open your mouth. You're not like most women."

I raise my eyebrow, "And how many women do you know?" I'm teasing him, that's one thing I don't want to know. I know he's not a saint, and I don't expect him to be, but I also don't want to know how many women he's been with, because knowing the truth is going to hurt.

He glances away, and my teasing has backfired. Great and now my mind is wondering about who he's been with and how many.

"Let's go in. I need to eat." I tell him as I turn in

his arms, but he stops me, "What's the matter?" I ask.

"The women I've been with don't matter Mia. I'm with you." His finger reaching up to my chin to make me look at him. "Mia, since that first night, I've not been with anyone. I knew then that you're the one for me."

My breath hitches at his admission. "Hudson." Tears sting my eyes, God, who knew he could be so freaking sweet?

His amber eyes flash with darkness. "Damn, I really need to get you upstairs. It's been too long since I've been inside you."

My mouth instantly dries, "You've just been inside my mouth, Hudson, I'm the one feeling short-changed." I smirk, as he grinds his jaw. "I need food." I lie, but he's teased me so much, it's time to repay the favor.

"Oh, you're going to pay Princess, just you wait and see." He whispers in my ear, "I'm going to spank you so hard you cum."

I squeeze my legs closed, God, why does he do this? I'm like a puddle of goo when he says those things to me.

"Now, let's eat before I forget you need to and take you upstairs." He growls as he places his hand on my lower back and leads me inside, he walks past the sitting room where both Harrison and Mom are seated and into the kitchen. He places the bag of McDonalds on the counter, he's been carrying it since we got out of the car, he went around the drive-thru because he wasn't getting out of the car and wouldn't let me go in by myself, I had to roll my eyes at that one. I get that he's macho, but there's no need to be over dramatic.

Taking a seat on the bar stools, Hudson reaches in the bag and passes me my chicken nuggets and fries. "Thank you," I tell him, and I'm rewarded with a soft smile, something he doesn't give very often. Usually when he smiles there's still that hardness to him, but not now, and I think it's my favorite look of his.

I take a bite of a chicken nugget and decide it's time to get to know Hudson, hell we should have done this a while ago, but better late than never. "Do you see your mom much?" I know that she's alive, seeing as Harrison and she were married when Mom and he got together, I'm actually shocked that Mom did that.

He nods as his mouth is currently occupied with a Big Mac. "Yeah, although I've not seen her in a couple of weeks." He tells me once he's able.

"Why? Do you get along?" I ask and pop a fry into my mouth.

His hand reaches out and touches my thigh. It's as if he can't be around me and not hold me in some way. I love it though. "She's bitter; I guess she has been for a while. She doesn't know what to do now that Dad's gone."

"How long were your parents married?" I ask and reach for another nugget.

"Just over thirty-two years." He replies, shaking his head.

"Were they happy?"

He laughs, "A fucking disaster, they shouldn't have been together. They argued day and night. They were miserable." He doesn't sound happy, and I'm wondering what I'm missing.

"But?"

His eyes raise in surprise, "You're astute." He comments and I smile at his words, "But, they were married, and they took vows, that's an honor they had to obey. Something that my ma took seriously. My dad on the other hand," He shakes his head. "As I said a fucking disaster."

I glance around just to make sure that no-one is eavesdropping, "Do you hate my mom for their marriage ending?" I saw the disapproval in Mom's eyes today, but Hudson's not once made me believe that he dislikes her.

He doesn't look at me, and finishes off his Big Mac before he answers me. "I don't blame her for their marriage ending." His tone deep and pissed off; he doesn't want to talk about this anymore.

I change the subject, noting that he never actually said if he hated Mom or not. "Is the club the only business you have?"

His body tenses, "Kind of, what about you, you're in college, what are you majoring in?"

Great, another question dodged. "I'm majoring in English."

He smirks, "You're a book nerd?"

"I'm a bibliophile. There's a difference."

He leans in, his lips inches from mine. "Oh yeah, so enlighten me. What is the difference?"

"A bibliophile is a lover of books, who also collects them." I feel my cheeks heating. I feel like a geek. "Whereas a book nerd is someone who always has their head stuck in a book, technically learning."

He stares at me in disbelief. "Princess." He murmurs and shakes his head.

"If you want to be technical about it, a nerd is

an unattractive, socially awkward, annoying, undesirable, and/or boring person."

His hand tightens on my leg, "You're not boring, annoying or socially awkward. You are definitely not undesirable. And the fucking opposite of unattractive."

I shrug, I don't think I'm ugly, but I'm not stunning.

"Fucking hell." He mutters, "Okay, Princess, let's get one thing straight. You're gorgeous, every fucking inch of you is. I should know I've seen every one of those inches." My breath catches at his words and I squeeze my legs tighter together. Why does he always do this to me?

"Understand?" He asks as his hand on my thigh adds pressure; he wants me to open my legs. That's not happening, not here where anyone could walk in and see us.

I nod and continue eating, I'm starting to get really tired, and I want to check in on Lacey. I sent her a couple of messages while we were driving back, she answered them saying she was fine, but I need to see it to believe it.

"What are you going to do after you finish college?" He asks after a few moments of silence.

I shrug, "I've not fully decided yet. I'd love to be

an English teacher or an editor." I throw the last of my fries into my mouth and reach for my Coke.

He studies me for a beat, "Editing? Is that something that you'd like to do? Teaching seems like it'll be more..." His head moves as if he's trying to find the right word to say, "Exhilarating... Rewarding even."

Placing my drink down on the counter, "Both editing and teaching would be rewarding, each in their own way. Take teaching, knowing that you could help a child is one of the most rewarding things in this world. Children, young adults are the future and if you can help them weave their own path, be a part in helping them become the best that they can be. That would be the best feeling in the world."

His gaze is intense, as he stares at me. It's like he's transfixed. He's hanging on my every word. This man gives me his full attention, and I love it. "What about editing?" He doesn't sound very convinced that it's worthwhile.

"Getting to edit someone's book, a book that they've poured their heart and soul into. Being a part of the process to take that diamond in the rough and make it into a shiny, polished one." I shake my head as goosebumps cover my body.

"Having a book you worked on hit the bestseller lists." I don't think I'm selling editing that much, I can't express the words as to what being an editor would mean.

"I see that you're passionate about both of them. Now, I have a question for you..." Oh shit, that sounds ominous. "Would you think about going to college here in Cali?"

My eyes widen, "Um, why?"

His eyes narrow, and I feel as though I've said the wrong thing. "Why?" He grits out, "I've been looking for you for almost two fucking years, I've finally got you, do you really think I'm letting you go?"

Oh... I have no idea what to say to that.

"Mia, what do you think we're doing here?" He asks sounding exasperated.

"I don't know Hudson, I have no idea what we're doing. You're the only person I've been with." I blurt out, I don't want him to think that I'm playing around, I'm not, I just don't have a clue as to what I should be doing. This relationship thing, if that's what we're doing, it doesn't come with a manual. I'm winging it.

He smiles at me and I'm pretty sure he's actually

laughing at me. "Princess, you're cute. So would you relocate?"

"Can I think about it?" That smile he had instantly vanishes. "I left Cali for a reason Hudson. Being here reminds me so much of what I've lost. I miss my dad every day and I left because I couldn't deal with the constant reminders." I want to go to his grave, I'll go when Lacey's home.

His eyes soften. "What about when you're here?"

I scoff, "God, there's not one bit of my dad in this house. A man my mom spent over fifteen years with. It's like he's been forgotten. I hate that my mom's wiped him from her life. It hurts that she doesn't think he deserves to be in her life. He's dead, and no matter if she didn't love him, they still had years together, good years together. Having one picture of us would show that she had a heart you know?" Tears sting my eyes, I didn't realize how much Mom hiding him has affected me.

I hear a gasp behind me and close my eyes. Great, Mom's heard everything.

"Princess." Hudson says low, his deep voice soothing and I open my eyes and see him staring at me, his amber eyes so full of worry.

Taking a deep breath, "I'm going to check in on

Lacey and then I'm going to bed. Meet you there?" I whisper as my fingers reach for his and I gently brush them with mine.

"Yep, I'll be up in a bit." He tells me and I'm wondering if he's going to say something to my mom? I don't want to talk to her just yet, especially as I'm so emotional. Tomorrow after I take Lacey to the airport I'll talk to her, we'll clear the air and everything will be okay.

I turn on my heel and walk past both Mom and Harrison, I wonder how long they've been listening for?

"Tina, leave her for tonight, you heard her, she's hurting. You'll only make things worse between you." Harrison tells her and I don't stop, I walk toward the stairs.

"She hates me." Mom says but I don't, right now I feel as though I don't know her anymore.

"She feels betrayed." Hudson's deep voice causes me to falter on the step, I carry on walking up them, but listen to what Hudson's saying. "She's right. Look around this house. There's not one picture of Mia's father, nor is there a picture of Mom."

"Son, we're starting a new life together. One where we're putting the past behind us." Harrison says and I sit on the top step and listen, as soon as I do, a door opens behind me. Glancing behind me, I realize that it's Lacey's door that's open.

"Does that include your children?" God, Hudson sounds angry.

"You okay?" I ask her as she sits beside me on the step.

She shrugs, her eyes red from crying. No she's not, but she will be.

"What's that supposed to mean?" Mom asks, her voice a shrill sound. She doesn't like Hudson and I'm curious as to why? As far as I know she only met him the night of their party. He's not done anything to warrant her not liking him.

Lacey lays her head against my shoulder and I wrap my arm around her. Pain hitting me as she begins to weep quietly against me. I wish I could help her but I can't. There's nothing I can do other than be here for her, offering her support.

"It means, this big pretentious house and not one picture of your daughter. Plenty of the two of you though. Fucking selfish." Hudson tells them, his voice is harder than I've ever heard it before. It's a different side to him, I can imagine his amber eyes darkening with anger.

"Son..." Harrison warns and I want to hide,

they shouldn't be arguing, not over something that I said.

"Dad, don't. Mia's told me how Tina didn't even tell her you two were getting married, nor that you were even thinking about it. Fuck Dad, she didn't even invite her to your damn wedding."

Lacey jumps at the harshness of Hudson's voice. He's shouting and I'm surprised that no one else has come out to hear what's going on. Barney and Jagger are here too. A loud thump makes me jump. Shit, this is getting bad. It's why I didn't want to say anything to Mom, I didn't want the arguments that come with the conversation we're inevitably going to have.

"Lacey, come on, let's get you to bed." I tell her as I get to my feet, my hands reaching for hers to help her up. She gingerly gets to her feet and we walk to her bedroom.

As soon as I walk into the room, I'm shocked by how the bed looks. It reminds me of how Hudson and I leave our bed in the morning. It looks like she's had sex. Glancing at her, the way her eyes are downcast and her ears are red tells me that maybe she did.

"Lacey?" I ask and as soon as I do she breaks down. "Oh Lacey, what happened?"

She sits on the bed, her head in her hands as she weeps quietly, "I was so stupid Mia."

Sitting beside her I pull her into my arms, "Why?"

"I don't know why I did it, I just wanted to feel anything other than this pain I'm in. It seemed like a good idea at the time." She weeps.

"What was it like?" I ask and she glances at me in shock, at least she's not crying in her hands anymore. "Well?"

She shakes her head, a small frown trying to form but she's biting it back. "Awful. I cried as soon as it was over."

My eyes widen. Holy hell, how bad could it have been? "What did Barney say?"

Her eyes narrow, "Nothing, he left as soon as it was over. That's what made me cry in the first place." Her tone has a bite to it.

What a jerk! How dare he?

"Lace, what the hell happened?" How did it go from her ignoring him, to him bedding her and walking away?

"He brought me home from the party. We didn't really say anything on the drive, but when we walked upstairs, he kissed me and things went from there. It happened really quickly, it was okay I guess. I mean I didn't come, he did and as soon as he did, he left."

Oh wow, he's a bigger jerk than I thought! Who takes advantage of a woman who's in the midst of grief? She just lost her grandmother, a woman who practically raised her.

"Oh Lacey, I'm so sorry." She must have really liked him, she wouldn't have had sex with him if she didn't. This is going to hurt her, it's the last thing she needed, especially after losing her grandmother.

"It's okay Mia. It's my own fault." She whispers.

"No." I tell her sharply, "It's not your fault. You had sex with a man, a grown-ass man. One that knew how vulnerable you were and the jerk left you afterward. That, Lace, isn't your fault. That's on him. It shows you that your time is better off spent elsewhere." I could kick that douche in the balls. How dare he do that to her?

"I'm tired, goodnight Mia." She tells me as she stands from the bed.

I sigh, today has been a shitty day for Lacey and there's nothing I can do to help her. "Okay Lace, goodnight. I'll see you in the morning." She doesn't say anything as I leave her room, as soon as I'm in the hall, the arguing from downstairs assaults my ears.

"She's my wife Hudson." Harrison yells and I'm wondering what's been said.

"Yeah Dad, I know, she's the only person you give a shit about."

I close my eyes, what's going on now is between Hudson and his dad. We're one big fucked-up family. I guess what they say is true, there's no such thing as perfect.

I walk upstairs and into my room, I cleaned it before I left this evening, the sheets have been changed. The bed looks so inviting. Stripping down to my underwear, I climb into bed and close my eyes. This day turned into one of the worst days I've had in a while. I need to sleep. Hopefully tomorrow will be somewhat better.

FIFTEEN

Hudson

When Mia spoke about her mom making it seem as though her dad didn't exist, it made me dislike her mom even more. So far all I've seen from Tina is how selfish she is. Everything is about her and what she wants. Fuck what's good for her daughter. Seeing them overhear what Mia and I were talking about pissed me off, finally my girl was opening up to me. Finally feeling comfortable around me to ask questions, some of which I had to dodge as now isn't the right time to be telling her what I do for a living. She's still unsure of what to do, not because of me but because she's never done anything like this before. Neither have I, but fuck that, I know what I want and I'm going after it, guns blazing if I need to.

Tina's standing at the door with her arms crossed, she doesn't look fucking upset that her daughter's not talking to her. "Son..." Dad begins, his tone trying to get me to back down. Not going to happen. Someone needs to set him right.

"Dad, don't. Mia's told me how Tina didn't even tell her you two were getting married, nor that you were even thinking about it. Fuck Dad, she didn't even invite her to your damn wedding."

Tina's eyes widen, yeah, she mustn't have thought Mia would have told anyone that. Dad rolls his eyes, he's not buying this, my hands slam down on the table. "Don't be stupid son, of course Tina told her about the wedding. Mia's upset, she's lashing out."

I let out a bitter laugh, "God, this is a joke coming from you. Dad, you should know by now how to spot a damn liar. Look at her." My voice is vibrating with anger.

"Tina?" Dad enquires but it doesn't take a fucking genius to see that she's been lying, the deer in the headlights look doesn't suit her. Her mouth's open in shock. "Tina?" Dad asks once again. He comes and sits down on the seat that Mia vacated. "Why Tina? That's your daughter. She deserved to know that we were getting married. You told me that she wasn't able to come to the wedding. That she was busy with college."

I laugh, "And you believed her? Christ Dad, what the hell happened to you?" I shake my head, actually disgusted that he's turned into this asshole. One thing I could always guarantee was my dad had a keen eye, he could always spot a liar, someone out for their own gain and he'd make sure that anyone who lied to him regretted it. Yet here he is with Tina, and he's looking at her as if she's done nothing wrong.

"Son, watch your mouth." He bites out and I get up and walk to the fridge, I need a damn drink. Christ, how can someone as sweet as Mia have Tina as her mom?

"Tina, what the hell?" Dad asks, "Son, pass me a beer too." Grabbing two beers, I pass him one and go and stand by the sink, keeping enough distance between Tina and me.

"Harrison, I didn't want to upset her, you saw how vulnerable she is. Any mention of her dad and it sets her off."

Bringing the bottle to my lips so that I don't say anything. She's full of shit and we all know it.

"Tina, why did you lie to me?" Dad's getting angry, he hates lies and Tina's full of them.

She shrugs, "I guess I didn't want everything to be about Rob." Tears fill her eyes and I want to roll mine, God, how does she think crying is going to make my dad believe her?

"Oh Tina, don't cry. Christ." He says through clenched teeth and is up out of his chair and pulling her into his arms within seconds.

Putting the bottle down on the counter, I clap. "Bravo, epic performance." I say snidely, Dad's eyes cut to me and narrow dangerously. "You're an even bigger fool than I thought. She's a liar and selfish, you're too blind to see it."

"She's my wife, Hudson." Dad shouts at me as his arms tighten around Tina.

I let out a bitter laugh, fucking typical Dad. "Yeah Dad, I know, she's the only one you give a shit about."

Dad releases Tina and grabs his beer, "Hudson, you're a grown man, you understand these things."

I throw my head back and laugh. "These things? What would those things be Dad?"

He grabs his beer, "You have your woman now, you know what it's like to want to protect them, to make sure that they're happy and safe."

I shake my head. It's time to get the hell out of this room before I lose my damn mind.

Grabbing my bottle off the counter, I walk past them both.

"Hudson, will you fucking talk to me?" Dad shouts as I reach the door.

Turning around, I face him, "Why the hell should I?"

"I'm your father, the least you could do is talk to me. What the hell is your problem?"

"My problem?" I scoff, "Where the hell should I start?" I ask rhetorically and watch as the venom in my voice takes him by surprise. He knows that I'm pissed but up until now I've not unleashed on him. He was the boss and I was respectful. That shit has changed.

"You are not the boss anymore, you have no fucking respect for me." I give him a pointed look, he doesn't even deny it. He keeps his head held high and stares at me, waiting for me to continue. "I don't like backseat drivers. You willingly gave up the title so you could marry." I spit the word out as I glare at Tina.

Dad laughs, "You're angry because I left you in charge?"

I smile, people have said that my smile causes them to run a mile. Dad falters and Tina takes a step backward. "No, I'm not angry that you left me in charge. We all know that I'm better at being the boss than you ever were. I'm disappointed that you left the family behind. That you gave in to petulant demands and gave up everything that your father had worked so hard to build."

He doesn't say anything because he knows what I'm saying is true.

"It wasn't a petulant demand. It was a serious request. I didn't want that life and I certainly don't want my daughter in that life." Tina states.

"Tina. Enough." Dad tells her, finally, he's understanding.

"But Dad, I'm angry at the way you treated my mom. The way you'd use her for your own personal punching bag. You want to know why Ma is so fucking low? Because you made her so. She's been physically and mentally abused for God knows how long and as soon as you find someone newer you finally set her free. It was a long time coming and it's something you should have done a long ass time ago." Each and every word I say is in pure and utter anger, years of watching my mom suffer at his hands. It's stopped but fuck, Ma is a mess. I don't know if she'll ever recover.

"Your mom let herself go, she wasn't the same woman after the miscarriage."

"Whose fault was that?" I shake my head, "You fucked up with her dad, you broke her. Make sure you don't do the same to Tina."

"He's never laid a finger on me." Tina tells me and it takes everything I have not to say anything back to her. "He wouldn't, your father is a changed man."

I nod, this is going nowhere, I've business to attend to. "Good for you."

"Son, I know you'll do better than I ever have. My actions showed you what not to do. If it means anything, I am truly sorry for not being your dad. You needed me to be your dad and not your boss."

"No, I needed you to be a decent human being and you weren't. You've made a lot of mistakes Dad, it's time to rectify those mistakes." Not wanting to waste any more breath on this pointless conversation. Dad looks like he's not going to change, Tina's attached to my dad like a viper, making him believe her lies. It's shit, and I'm not getting into it anymore. I've said my piece and that's it.

Walking upstairs, I walk into my dad's office, he's told me that it's mine to use while I'm here. Jagger, Martin, and Barney are waiting for me, Jagger has a smile on his face, the fucker has a twinkle in his eye. Barney's jaw's clenched, whatever the fuck happened has pissed him off. Martin is sitting tall, his shoulders squared as he waits patiently for me.

"Barney, what's up?" I ask as I take a seat at the desk.

"Nothing Boss." He instantly replies. Whatever has pissed him off is personal and he's not talking.

I nod once, "Jagger?" I ask with a smirk, he's grinning like a loon.

"Just waiting to see if what I've put into motion works out, Boss." Again, it's personal, I have a feeling I know what he's done and I hope it works out for him.

"Okay, Martin?" I ask and his hand reaches into his pocket and he pulls out a sheet of paper. "What?" I ask, I'm on edge now, he's not said a word since I've walked into this office.

"Matt and Carmine did in fact put Ulric's body in a construction site in Barstow. They hid their tracks really well. It's taken me this long to make sure they did it." He tells me but that's not what's got him rigid. There's something more.

I nod, maybe they're not as useless as I first believed. "And?"

He hands me the sheet of paper and I read it.

. . .

Mr Brady,

You're not as smart as you think you are.

I know that it was you that had my cousin deported.

For that you will pay. This is just the beginning.

Shit, fucking Juan.

"How did he find out?" My teeth clench at the thought of some fucker betraying me and telling this scumbag that I had his fucking cousin deported.

"I'm working on finding out. Boss, that note was attached to Jorge." He glances at Jagger, whose smile has now vanished, replaced with his dark look.

"What do you mean attached to Jorge?" My temper rising as both Martin and Barney glance at the floor. "Someone better open their fucking mouth and start talking." I say through gritted teeth.

"Jorge's body was found at the back of the club last night. The asshole pinned that to his body." Jagger tells me, shaking his head as he does so. "Fucking tortured him Boss. There's scorch marks on his hands and feet. Ones I've seen before."

I know what he's telling me. The scorch marks tell us he was electrocuted. He may have been the leak but my gut is screaming that it wasn't him. That someone else ratted me out and there's only a select few that knew what my plans were, that was two of the men in this room, Jorge, a police officer, and the damn immigration officer. Someone spilled their guts and when I find out who, I'm going to sew their mouth shut and make them wish they were never born.

"Martin, find out who snitched." I tell him and he instantly gets to his feet. "Your sole duty is to find out who the leak is." He nods once and leaves the room.

I glance at Jagger, he too will be finding out. He's the only one I trust implicitly not to betray me.

"Barney, tomorrow morning, you'll be driving us to the airport. Lacey is flying out tomorrow."

His jaw tightens even more and if he continues he'll break the fucking thing. "Yes Boss." He too gets to his feet and leaves.

"What do you need Hudson?" Jagger knows me too well.

"Someone snitched. There were five people who knew that I set Arturo's deportation in motion. One of those people just left the room. Make sure he's not the one."

Shock registers on his face. "Boss, are you sure?"

"I'm not sure who I trust, so I need you to make sure that he's not betraying me."

"How do you know I wasn't the leak?" He asks and sounds insulted.

I smirk, "You're a lot of things Jag, but you would never betray me."

He looks confused at my comment but nods, "I'll find out for you."

I nod, "How's things between you and Sarah?"

He sighs, "She's making everything about Allie. Anytime I broach the subject of us, she changes it around to say how much Allie is going to love to see me. It's going to be a challenge getting her back into my bed. But you know me Hudson." He smiles widely.

"You never back down from a challenge. Now get the hell out of here, it's time for me to go and see my woman."

The fucker smirks, "See you tomorrow Boss." And walks out of the office.

Just as I'm about to get up off the chair, Dad walks in. "Son, do you have a minute?"

"Sure, what's up?" Mia's going to be asleep before I even get up there.

He sits down in the chair that Jagger just vacated. "I've come to realize just how great at being the boss you are."

I raise my brow, that's some admission. One I never thought he'd make.

"You're great at masking things Hudson, you had me fooled for years. I honestly believed that you were fine with the way things were between your mom and me."

I roll my eyes, fucking hell I didn't realize he was a moron. "You were the boss, respect is everything and while I was a soldier, that was my job. To respect your position. I didn't respect you as a dad, or a husband, but I did as the boss."

"I was the same person." He tells me and I scoff, "Hudson, I'm trying to make amends."

Right, of course he is. I'm wondering why now? "Dad, you were the boss and it was expected of you to be an asshole. You have to be the meanest sonofabitch there is but also a fair one to your soldiers. That was who you were there, not who you should have been at home. You should never, lay a finger on a woman in anger. Never make them so low they contemplate ending their own life and you never disrespect them by cheating on them. You did all three, you weren't a father to me at all. Hell, I can't even remember you being a dad. You were the boss."

His jaw tenses and his nostrils flare, yeah, this anger is what I'm used to, although he's trying to contain it. "I fucked up, with you and with your mom. I'm hoping that you'll let me prove to you that I'm a changed man."

I bite back the sarcastic retort. "Okay."

"I want to start with your mom, do you think she'll be up to seeing me?" He questions, he actually looks sincere, his hands wringing together almost as if he's nervous.

"How about not yet? Ma's trying to get better, seeing you again is going to send her spiralling." I'm not going to let him hurt her anymore. Once she's on her feet and strong enough, then he can apologize.

"I'm proud of you Hudson." His voice hard, almost as if it hurts to say those words. "Proud of the man that you've become. I have no fucking idea how you became so amazing, it sure as shit wasn't me or your mother. As you said we were a fucking disaster."

So the asshole was listening from pretty much the beginning. Jackass. "You both showed me what not to do." I shrug, when you despise something enough, you'll do everything in your power to make sure you don't become them.

He laughs, "At least we showed you something." He shifts in his seat, sitting up a bit straighter. I know that pose, he's got something to say, and whatever he's about to say is going to piss me off. "Son, I know that you and Tina haven't gotten off on the right foot. I'm asking you to, please, bury the hatchet and start fresh. She's not who you believe her to be."

I roll my eyes, "She put you up to this?"

"No, Christ Hudson, you really are a suspicious fucker aren't you? No, she didn't put me up to it, I told her that if she continues with her hostility towards you, I'll divorce her." My eyes widen at his admission. "You're my son Hudson, I may be an asshole but you're my fucking son. No one treats you with disrespect. But, that doesn't mean you can be an asshole to her."

I huff out a breath, "Fine, I'll be nice."

Although, if she says one thing to upset Mia, all bets are off.

He gets to his feet, "Thanks son."

I stand, it's time to go and see Mia. "Don't thank me Dad, we'll see how things go."

He nods sharply as he leaves the room, I won't promise anything.

Leaving the office, I hear crying, my eyes glance to the room on my right. Barney's standing outside, his hand on the door handle. "You going in?" Obviously Lacey's crying, so why is he standing there?

He shakes his head, "No, I've done enough damage to her already." He tells me and walks into his room.

I'm not in the mood to try and decipher his cryptic bullshit. I turn and walk up the stairs, Lacey's soft cries following me as I do so. As soon as I open the bedroom door, Mia's soft snores greet me. Damn it. Glancing at the bed, I smile, her leg's peeking out from under the sheets, she's weird. I've noticed that when she sleeps she has to have one of her feet out of the sheets, she told me she gets too warm otherwise. Stepping into the room, I close the door behind me and lock it. Stripping down to my boxer shorts, I climb into the bed beside Mia. As soon as I do, she turns into me, her head coming to rest against my shoulder.

The fact that she seeks me out while she's asleep tells me that she's as deep in this as I am. Soon, I'll tell her everything. I just hope she's deep enough with me to accept it.

SIXTEEN

Hudson

Awkward. That's all I can use to describe the mood in this room. We're all sat around the kitchen table. Dad's talking, trying to keep everyone engaged but it's not working. Lacey and Barney are looking everywhere but at each other, Jagger's sitting there with a damn smile on his face. Whatever he has planned must be going his way, that fucker's never looked so happy. Mia's keeping her head down, she's sad, her best friends going home and she's still not ready to talk to her mom. Glancing at Tina, she's doing the exact same as Mia, head down focused on their breakfast. Not making eye contact with anyone else in the room.

The sound of my cell ringing, interrupts the silence. Tina's glance is one of wariness, whereas

Dad, Jagger, and Barney all shift in their seats. All sit a bit taller, they're on edge, this call could indicate anything. Usually if it's anything trivial, my men would call Martin or Jagger, when I'm getting a call it means something serious seeing as my closest men are here with me. Reaching into my pocket, I pull my cell out and see that it's Aaron calling me. Shit, he's the one who manages my bar. He's trustworthy to a certain extent. He owes me his life, and he's been loyal so far.

Getting to my feet, I leave the room. The heat of my men's stares hot on my back. They're uneasy, they'll not settle until they know what's happened. "What?" I answer the phone and instantly hear his deep breathing. "What happened?" I ask after he doesn't answer me, there's a sharpness to my voice.

"Boss, Carmine's been shot."

A buzzing sounds in my ears as my anger rises. "How is he?"

Aaron doesn't answer right away, "It doesn't look good Boss. He'll be lucky to make it through the day."

Fuck. "Who did it?"

"I don't know Boss, they broke into his house and shot him."

Shit, "How the fuck did they manage to break into his house? Where were Vi and the girls?"

"Vi found him, she had just left the girls at her mom's. Something about date night."

Thank fuck for that. "Where are you now?" I ask him, I need to get back to San Fran, and find out who the hell shot Carmine. This has Juan written all over it.

"I'm at the hospital Boss, as are some of the other men. Vi's not doing too good. She's had to be sedated."

Christ, "Okay, I'll be home in a few hours. Get the men to find out what the fuck happened. Stay vigilant." I warn him, that's too many of my fucking men dead. This shit stops now. I end the call, seething. My gut is screaming that it's Juan who shot Carmine and if he didn't do the deed himself, he orchestrated it.

"Martin." I say, slightly raising my voice but not enough that the entire house will hear me.

"Yes Boss." He answers immediately, appearing from the dining room.

I nod my head toward the room he just exited and he dutifully follows me inside. "Martin. Carmine has been shot. Have the plane ready to go.

Once Lacey's gone, We'll bring Mia back and leave."

Martin's face is straight but the tick in his left eye tells me that he's spitting mad. You don't fuck with our family and as much as Carmine is a lazy fuck, he's family. "Okay Boss, I'll organize the plane. Should be ready to leave in five. If the girls are ready?"

I nod, "They'll be ready." I assure him.

Voices sound, that means breakfast is finished, time to wrap this up.

"Do we know who shot Carmine?" His voice low as he glances at the door, he too heard the talking.

I shake my head, "The men are looking into it. If they've not found out by the time I'm back, you'll take over." I tell him, he's the man that gets me every bit of information I need.

Looking at him, you wouldn't think he was anything other than a nerdy bodyguard. He's not as muscular as the rest of us but that means shit. He's an animal when he gets going. He's my go-to man for when I need some information extracted from someone. He's made a name for himself, most of the time he just needs to threaten what he'll do and he'll have his prey singing like a canary.

"Son?" Dad calls out, he's close, no doubt he's waiting outside.

"Yeah?" I ask as I walk out into the hall, everyone's gathered around waiting for me. "Lacey are you ready to go?" That woman's eyes are red raw, I'm wondering if she slept at all last night.

She nods, her gaze moving from me to Barney who's looking anywhere but at her.

"Let's go." Jagger smiles as he claps his hands together, making Mia roll her eyes, but she too has a smile on her face. So much is different between them now, when she first saw him she wanted to kick him in the balls.

Jagger leads Mia and Lacey outside, Barney stares at their retreating backs, his eyes swirling with anger. I don't have time for his shit, he needs to get himself together. He's needed here, especially while I'm gone. I'll need him to keep an eye on Mia, as both Jagger and Martin will be with me, he's the only other person I trust to keep her safe. I turn to my dad, he's whispering something to Tina, she didn't even say goodbye to Mia.

Leaving the house, I walk to the car, Jagger's climbing into the front passenger side. Turning to look behind me, Martin's following behind, his cell in his hand and he's talking to someone. Good, he's organizing the plane.

The ride to the airport is a silent one. Not one person says a damn word. As much as I love peace and quiet, I dislike the mood that Mia's in, this shit needs to stop. She needs to talk to her mom and get it over and done with. Right now she's standing outside the airport talking to Lacey.

"Boss, the plane will be ready in an hour." Martin tells me as he drums his fingers on the steering wheel.

I nod, "Great. Call..." Vibrations shoot through my leg as music rings out from my pocket. Pulling out my cell, Aaron's name flashes on the screen. Ice chills my blood as I answer it. "Is he alive?"

Silence. That's what I'm greeted with. Fuck. "No Boss, he coded and they couldn't bring him back."

I swallow hard. "Find me who killed him. I don't give a fuck who you have to off to do it, just find me the person who shot him." My nostrils flare, as I try and keep my breathing even. I'm ready to kill someone. How dare they shoot my man and end his life. Fucking asshole.

"Yes Boss. I'll spread the word." He replies instantly.

"Aaron, put Vi and the girls up in a safe house. Until this fuck is found. No woman or child is to be left alone. Understood?"

"Yes Boss, I'll do it myself." His voice is as hard as mine. We all take this seriously, you don't fuck with our family.

"I'll be there soon." I tell him and hang up. Now to tell Mia that I won't be around for the next few days. I hope that it's days and not weeks.

"Fuck Hudson, what the hell is happening? Why do we need the plane and who died?" Jagger's voice is full of irritation, he hates to be left out of the loop.

"I've not had a chance to tell you yet. Carmine was shot, Aaron called me to tell me that he died. We've yet to find out who pulled the trigger but the guys are working on it. We're flying home because it's where I'm needed."

He nods, "We're going to find out who killed him." It's a promise.

"Hell yes we are, whoever it is, when I'm finished with them, they're going to regret going after my man." I give a sinister smile, I'm looking forward to enacting revenge. "Not one word to Mia though. I've yet to tell her anything. I've been waiting for the right time and it hasn't arisen yet. I'll tell her everything once we've found this motherfucker."

They nod once, they understand. "What are you doing about Sarah and Allie?" I ask Jagger, I keep my gaze on both Lacey and Mia, they're hugging and crying. Why the hell do women do that shit?

"She's holding out, I'm going to New York next month, I'm giving it time for both Sarah and Allie to get used to me, but once I'm there, I'm not leaving without them." He tells me with a wide smile.

I nod, that's good, it'll mean they're safe. Jagger won't let anything happen to either of them. "What about Carina? What are you going to do about her?" He's not said anything about her, hell he hasn't even told me that she left the rehab center and is currently back home with her parents.

"Leave Carina to me." His voice has an edge to it. "She won't get the chance to cause trouble."

"She always causes trouble. It's her middle name Jag. She's not going to let you, Sarah, and Allie be happy. She's going to go crazy. Fucking crazier than she's ever been before." That bitch is unstable at the best of times. She treats Jag like he's her property, anytime those two break up, she marks her territory. Something that Jagger should have nipped in the bud as soon as it happened.

A heavy sigh escapes him, "I know Hudson, God, she's the fucking devil in disguise. That woman was sweet as pie, and then bang." He snaps his fingers, "Turned into a motherfucking headache. She's being cut loose Hudson, I've told her parents, she leaves me alone or she's dead. I'm not playing around anymore. She does one more thing and I'm going to lose the damn plot."

What he means is if she does anything to Sarah or Allie he's going to lose the plot. If she does, it's her funeral. He'll slit her throat without a second thought. Jagger feels the same way about Sarah as I do about Mia. You don't fuck with our women, if you do, it'll be the last thing you do.

The back door to the car opens and Mia climbs in. Her eyes are filled with tears as she scoots all the way over so that her body is pressed against mine. "You okay?" I ask as I put my arm around her shoulder, pulling her even closer to me.

She nods against me, "Yeah, I wish she wasn't alone but there's not much I can do. I offered to travel with her but she said she wanted to be alone." So much sadness in her voice.

"It'll be okay Princess."

She huffs out a breath, "Yeah it'll be okay, there's nothing we can do about death except to put it aside and try and forge a path without them."

What do you say to that? My hand tightens around her shoulder as Martin drives off into the traffic.

"Hey Mia..." Jagger says and I can hear the smile in his voice. "Have you spoken to Sarah today?"

"No, why?" She sounds miserable and I fucking hate it.

"She'll cheer you up." Jagger tells her with a soft smile.

She sighs, but reaches for her cell and Facetimes Sarah. "Hey, how's Allie?" Mia asks as Sarah answers. She's not moved from her position against me.

Sarah's smile is bright, "She's really good, she's sleeping better now." Sarah beams, "I've finally been able to get some sleep."

Mia sits up, "Aww such a good girl." The pride in her voice makes Jagger smile.

"I know, she's amazing. How are you? I've missed you so much." Sarah says and there are tears in her eyes. "How's Lacey?"

Mia shakes her head, "Not good. she was

hurting last night and that fucker Barney didn't help matters." Mia growls.

Sarah raises her eyebrow in question, "Who's Barney, and what did he do?" Damn, what is it with these women? They get this vicious look in their eyes.

"Barney works for Hudson, or his dad. I'm not really sure. He just seems to always be around." Mia comments and I bite the inside of my cheek so I don't laugh.

"Okay, so he's a creeper. What did he do to Lacey?" Sarah asks, her tone has a bite to it, Jagger turns in his seat, so he's looking at us from the front.

"So, Lacey found out about her grandmother at the party last night. Barney was there and gave her a ride home." Mia tells her as she sinks back against me. "So Hudson and I hung out a bit, I knew she was safe," She shrugs, as if she feels that she did something wrong by staying with me instead of going home with Lacey. "When I was going to bed, I spoke to her. She was shattered Sarah. That big jerk had sex with her!"

I smirk, she's making out as if having sex is a bad thing.

Sarah gasps, "He didn't? They had sex? But she

was way too upset to do that! I spoke to her last night."

Mia nods, "I know that. Look Lacey's not entirely innocent. She wanted it as much as he did. But having sex after finding out that her grandmother, the woman who practically raised her, has died isn't right. Lacey was vulnerable."

Sarah's nose is turned up in disgust. "What did Lacey say?"

"She was so upset. After he had sex with her, he left. Like literally pulled out of her and left." The venom in Mia's voice tells me that Barney had better watch his back, if Mia had her way, she'd have his balls on a platter.

"He did not?" Sarah gasps, "Why?" She shakes her head, "Why are men assholes?"

"Not all of us." Jagger says and I glance at him, the fucker has a smile on his face.

"Hmm, coming from the man that kissed another woman hours after Sarah left your bed. That makes you an asshole." Mia tells him emphatically.

"Every single man is an asshole." Sarah says, "Look at Hudson, hell he didn't even know Mia's name the night he took her virginity."

"Sarah!" Mia gasps with outrage.

Sarah raises her hands, "Sorry, but it's true." She tells her sheepishly. "He was an asshole, you've all been one in some way or another, but it's how you redeem yourself that counts. Hudson, the way you care for Mia, more than makes up for the way things between you began."

I nod, "Thanks." I'd lay down my life for Mia.

"We got off-topic." Mia tells her as she reaches for my hand and gives it a squeeze. "What are we going to do about Lacey?"

Sarah nods, "Not much we can do right now. When she's back, we'll have a girls night. She'll need cheering up."

"Sounds good, as long as that goddaughter of mine is there. That little baby makes everyone smile."

"Wait, she was christened already?" Jagger's voice is full of hurt.

Mia huffs, "No. I call myself her godmother but Sarah doesn't want me to be."

Sarah's eyes widen. "I never said I don't want you to be, I just didn't want her christened without her dad."

Mia sits up straight, "So does that mean I'll be godmother?" Sheer excitement in her voice.

"Of course." Jagger tells her immediately.

"Really?" Both Sarah and Mia ask in unison.

Jagger rolls his eyes and snatches the phone out of Mia's hand, "Yes, Mia is your best friend, you've told me that she's been there for you since you were in school, that without her you'd have suffered."

"Jesus, you two really did talk." Mia quips, "Okay, so I'm godmother, who's godfather?"

"Hudson." Jagger answers again.

"Um, do I get a say?" Sarah asks.

"The next one you do."

Mia laughs, and I love that sound.

"Okay there big boy, you're getting way ahead of yourself. Just because I agreed to you coming here doesn't mean anything, we're not going there." There's no heat in Sarah's words whatsoever.

"Never say never." Jagger replies, the fucker has that million-dollar smile on his face.

"I've got to go, tell Mia, I'll call her later."

"Love you." Mia shouts so that she can be heard.

"Love you too. Call you later." Sarah tells her and the line goes dead.

"She's happy." Mia breathes as Jagger passes her phone back to her.

"Yeah Princess, she seems happy." I reply quietly.

She places a kiss against my lips, her face is brighter than I've seen it for days. She's lighter today, let's just hope it lasts.

My gut is screaming the closer we get to my dad's house, it has to be at the thought of leaving Mia. She'll be safe here, I know that, Barney will be here as will my dad. No one can get to her while she's here and that's the main thing. If I thought for one second she wasn't safe, there's no way I'd leave her. She needs to be with her mom right now, she needs to fix their relationship. As much as I dislike Tina, she's Mia's mom and the only parent she has left, so they need to patch things up. I just hope Tina realizes that her daughter needs her and not to be a bitch.

Martin pulls into my dad's drive, Mia's car is parked in front of the house instead of at the side where it had been parked when we left. Getting out of the car, the front door opens and Barney walks out. "Boss, your dad and Mrs. Brady have gone on an impromptu vacation." He informs me and my gut screams louder.

"Mom's gone?" Mia's whisper is harsh and I turn to face her, shit, she's got tears swimming in her eyes.

"Seems so Princess," I tell her softly, her arms wrap around her stomach. "Mia, get a bag packed."

Her eyes widen in surprise, "What? Why?" She questions and Barney steps away from us and toward the car.

"Mia, I have to go back to San Francisco today, something's come up with the club and I'm needed there. So please, pack a bag and come with me." I say, my gut's screaming and that means something is going to happen.

She glances around before her eyes land back on me, reaching for my hand she leads me inside of the house. "Hudson, these past few days have been amazing. Things between us are going a bit too fast though. Go home, sort out whatever it is you need to and then come back to me. Okay?"

Shit, "Mia..."

She shakes her head. "So much has happened since I've been here and I need some time to think. Just give me a little time. Please." She begs, her eyes pleading with me to listen to her.

I go against my better judgment. "Okay, but Mia, if you change your mind. Call me, you'll be by my side within hours. Okay?"

Her hands go to my face, the softness a stark contrast to the roughness of my stubble. "I promise you Hudson, I'll call if I change my mind." She leans up on her tiptoes and presses her lips against mine. "Is it weird that I'm going to miss you?" She asks in a quiet voice.

"God no, I'm going to miss the fuck out of you." I confess, I shouldn't be leaving her, not when she'll only have Barney as back up.

"I'll call and text, you're not getting rid of me that easily." She smiles and my gut settles a bit. "What time are you leaving?"

"Now, there's a plane waiting for me." I tell her as I pull her into my arms. Her body feels great against mine and my dick starts to stir as it does every time she's in close proximity.

"Already?" She pouts.

"Damn, you're cute." I tell her with a smile. "I'm hoping I'll be gone a couple of days tops." I promise her.

"Okay." She breathes as I place a hard kiss against her lips.

"See you soon Princess." I tell her as I release her.

"Bye." Her voice is soft and willowy.

I wink at her and leave the house, it's taking every inch of self-control to leave her where she is. "Anything happens to her, I'm holding you personally responsible." I tell Barney as I reach the car.

He stands up straight and looks me dead in the eye. "I'll guard her with my life Boss. She's yours and that means she's ours. Nothing will happen to her. Not while she's with me."

"Good, I'll call you later." I get into the car, my eyes glance to the front door, Mia's standing there with her arms crossed. A lone tear falls down her face and I feel like a fucking ass, she shouldn't be by herself but she needs time, if that time makes her realize that she's mine then so be it. She's getting a couple of days, that's it. Then I'm coming for her.

SEVENTEEN

Mia

It's been six days, six days since Hudson got into the car and left. Six days of being in this monstrosity of a house with only a jerk to keep me company. A jerk that doesn't talk, not that I want to talk to him. Not after the way he treated Lacey. Lacey hasn't answered any calls from Sarah or I. I'm worried about her, she's texted me telling me she's okay, that she needs time and she'll call me when she's ready. That was three days ago and I'm hoping she'll call soon.

Mom arrived back last night, we still haven't really spoken. A quick hello and that was it. Today, though, today is the day that we have that discussion. I'm worried but at the same time, I've missed my mom, we've never had a falling out like this before and it hurts. It killed me not having her to talk to, not having her to laugh with. That's something that I could always count on, no matter what crappy day I was having, Mom would always be there. I need to find out why she lied, why she thought it was okay not to invite me to the wedding and why she broke up a marriage.

Hudson, God, that man sure knows how to make me love him and I *do* love him. These past few days have shown me just how much I care about him, how much I want to be with him. Everything about him is amazing and I'm truly head over heels in love with him. So much so that I've spent the last couple of days researching colleges here in California, I wanted to make sure that if I were to move back here that I did it for all the right reasons. I found a college in San Francisco that actually has a great English course, it's highly recommended and I've applied to start next semester there. It's not just because of Hudson, although he is a major factor, but Sarah's told me that she may come home. It would be amazing if she did. I've not told anyone my decision yet but my mind is made up and I'm happy with it.

My cell rings and Hudson's name is on the caller ID. "Hey you, you okay?" I ask as I do every time he calls hoping that today is the day he says he'll be back.

"Yes Princess, I'm okay, I'm hoping to be with you tomorrow." It's the same thing he tells me every day. It's a running joke now between us.

"Okay Hudson." I say softly and he groans which makes me smile.

"Princess, you know what that breathy voice does to me. I just wanted to check in with you and see how you are doing?" He growls sending shivers down my spine.

"I'm okay, Mom got home last night so we'll be talking today."

He makes a humming sound. "That's good Mia, it's time you two sorted your shit out."

"Yeah," I sigh, I'm actually dreading it. "I'm not sure I'm ready for it but it has to be done. What do you have planned for today?"

He laughs, "Nothing as daunting as what you have planned." Voices sound in the background, "Princess I've got to go, I'll call you later."

"Okay Hudson, I love you." My eyes widen as I realize what I've just said.

"Mia..." He rumbles, "You don't get to say that when I'm not beside you."

My tongue darts out and wets my lips, "Hudson." I moan, not sure what to say.

"Mia." He whispers, "I wanted to say it to your face."

"Say it now." I whisper back, a smile on my lips.

"I love you Princess and you're going to find out just how much when I get back to you."

My heart melts at his admission. "I love you too Hudson, but please, hurry up and come back. I miss you like crazy."

"I know, I'll be there soon. I promise." He's promised before and he's still not here.

"Okay, I'll talk to you later." I say not wanting him to know that I don't believe him.

"Definitely. Later Princess." He ends the call and I still have a smile on my face. I've never felt as happy as I am now. Hudson has made me the happiest I've ever felt in my life.

Getting off the bed, I make my way to the door, "Mia?" I hear my mom call.

"Yeah Mom?" I call back as I begin to make my way downstairs.

She waits until I get to the bottom step, "Is it okay to talk?"

I give her a soft smile, "Yeah Mom, of course."

Relief washes through her, "Can we go out onto the deck?"

I nod, "Yeah, it's a nice day." I follow behind her as she leads the way, awkwardness fills the gap between us, I'm not sure if one talk is going to clear the air but I'm hoping it will help. There's a pitcher of iced tea and chocolate brownies on a plate, she's been waiting for me, I like the gesture of her wanting to make it informal but I'm too nervous. The sooner this chat is out of the way the better.

"Did you and Harrison have a nice vacation?" I ask, hoping to start on something easy and work toward the harder stuff.

She reaches for the pitcher, "Yes, it was nice to get away, I think all of us needed the break, the time apart. It gave me time to think, time to get what I need to say properly, I don't want to hurt you Mia, and the last time we talked I did and for that I'm forever sorry." Sincerity dripping from her every word.

She pours us both drinks and I take one from her. "I know you didn't mean to hurt me Mom, and I get what you were trying to say. It was just too much. Everything had changed and then you told me you and Daddy weren't in love. It felt as though everything I had known was a lie. That hurt and hearing you say you regretted having me even though it's not what you meant made all of that worse." I'm glad that we're trying to sort things out, "I shouldn't have got mad, you told me how you felt and I shouldn't have gotten mad. I'm sorry Mom."

She reaches for my hand, "Don't apologize Mia, you didn't do anything wrong. How are you and Hudson getting along?" There's a bite to her tone, she really doesn't like Hudson and I'm not really sure why.

"We're good Mom, I miss him." I tell her honestly, "I've been doing a lot of thinking, as Sarah may be coming home and things with Hudson are going well, I've applied for college in San Francisco, I want to be close by, I miss Sarah and Allie. I want to be close to you, to Dad." I hate that I've not visited him since I've been gone. Hell, I've yet to visit him since I've been here, but that's going to change. I'm going to go this week, spend some time in Oakland, be closer to my dad.

Mom's eyes widen in surprise. "Really?"

I nod, "Yeah Mom."

She smiles, "Okay, so giving you these means so much more."

Frowning, I'm confused. "Giving me what?"

She reaches into her pocket, "These." She tells

me as she pulls a set of keys out of it. That shoehorn keyring makes me smile, I bought it for Dad for Father's Day one year, it was such a goofy present but he didn't care. He carried it every day with him, treasured it as if it were the best present in the world.

"Mom." I whisper, is she doing what I think she is?

"I spoke to Harrison, I told him that I wanted to take the house off the market and give it to you. He agreed, thinking it was the perfect thing to do. It'll be transferred into your name soon. But it's yours to do as you want with."

Tears spring to my eyes, I can't believe it. "Thank you." I say hoarsely, trying not to cry.

"Maybe if Lacey wants to switch colleges too, she could live with you?"

I like that idea, "Yeah, and I was thinking if Sarah does come home, that she and Allie could move in with me too."

Mom's face lights up. "You are your father's daughter Mia, you want everyone you love to be close. I think having your girls with you is a wonderful idea. But it also means you'll be close for me to visit you."

"Always Mom, you know that." It's true. I'd love

to have her around me, she'll only be a couple of hours away from me instead of the ten that we're currently apart while I've been living in Arizona. "Okay, Mom, I want to ask you something."

Her face falls, "You're going to ask about Hudson's mom."

I nod, "I couldn't believe that you got with Harrison while he was married, Mom. That's not who I thought you were."

"When I first met Harrison, you'd gone to college. I was alone in a house that used to be so filled with love. As much as your father and I weren't *in* love with each other, he was my best friend, Mia. I loved him like that and him dying hurt, it pained me and watching you break hurt even more."

Tears slip down my face, and I wipe them away, God, I hate talking about Dad dying. It feels like yesterday that I was told. It's the worst thing in the world and I never want to hear the words, 'I'm sorry, he's dead' again.

"Mia, I was lonely. I went to a bar and tried dating, but nothing was helping. My loneliness was consuming me. Until I met Harrison." Her eyes light up as a smile forms on her lips. She truly is happy, and I can't fault her for falling in love with him. I don't think I've ever seen her this happy.

"I didn't know he was married. I got to know him, I was drawn to him. I can't explain it; it's like he's a magnet, pulling me toward him. By the time the truth had gotten out, that he was married, I was in deep Mia. I knew that he was the man I wanted to spend the rest of my life with. That he was my one."

"So what did you do?" I ask. I understand what she means, what she's described about how she feels about Harrison is exactly what I'm feeling with Hudson, so I can't fault her for that. I don't think I could give Hudson up but if he was married, that would change things.

The smile she gives me is a weak one. "I made a mistake Mia. I should have told him no more when I found out about Paula. But I was weak, being with Harrison, it brought back the real me, the woman I had lost. So I continued seeing him until, eventually, he came to the decision to divorce Paula and for us to get married."

I feel bad for her. I don't think I can be mad at her, I'm not sure what I'd have done in her situation. "Okay, Mom, I understand. I think it was the wrong decision, but there's nothing that can be done about it now."

She nods, "I think that's why Hudson dislikes me." Her tone once again has that bite to it that she gets whenever she talks about Hudson.

I sigh, "Mom, please don't." I beg. I don't want to get into it about Hudson.

"Look, Mia, there are things about him that you don't know. He's not a good man." She says, her eyes flashing with anger.

"Mom, I know Hudson, he's a good man. Please don't do this. I don't want to argue again."

She doesn't listen. "Mia, that man is dangerous. He's a drug dealer for crying out loud."

I laugh, "Yeah okay Mom." I roll my eyes, the lengths she's going to, just so that we won't be together. It's ridiculous.

"Mia," She tells me, and I look at her. I mean really look at her, her eyes so full of worry. Whatever she's about to say, I know that I'm not going to like it. "Mia, Hudson owns Synergy, it's a front as such. He's the drug Kingpin. His dad was one before him and his grandfather before that. When Harrison proposed to me I said yes on one condition. That he'd leave that life and he did, but in doing so, he passed the title onto Hudson. Mia,

Hudson is a dangerous man, not that I think he'd hurt you in any way but the life he leads could. Please listen to me." She pleads with me.

I sit here in stunned silence, what am I meant to do with this information? Hudson never once told me anything about this, he's gone out of his way to keep this from me.

"Mia, baby, talk to me."

My throat lodges, I have no idea what I'm thinking or feeling. "He's never once said anything bad about you." I whisper, "He may hate you Mom, but he's never once shown me that." I want her to know the Hudson I know. I don't know why, but I think it's important, "He's always saying that I need to talk to you, make things right between us."

"Mia?" Mom breathes.

"Every chance you've got, you've tried to bring him down." A lone tear falls from the corner of my eye down my face and onto my top lip. "He doesn't deserve your hatred."

"Mia, that man is a drug dealer. There's nothing I wouldn't do to protect you." She says vehemently.

I'm not listening to her. I'm so hurt that she's trying to turn me against Hudson. "He's the man I love," I whisper. I'm so scared. What do I do?

"He's a killer." She spits out, "That man kills people."

My eyes widen, "What?"

She shakes her head in disgust. "Mia, he supplies drugs to everyone, including children. He has no problem using a gun to deal with his problems."

The walls are closing in on me; I need to breathe. This is too much. Pushing away from the table, I snatch the keys off it and get to my feet. I need to get out of here. Running into the house, I rush past Harrison and make my way to the front door, just as I place my hand on the handle I hear shouting.

"What the fuck is wrong with you?" Harrison shouts, but I don't stay around to hear Mom's response. I rush to my car and get in, starting it up, the motor purrs to life, and I get the hell out of there.

God, I'm stupid. There was always something about Hudson that screamed at me, but I put it down to my naivety. He was my first, and I thought that I wasn't well versed in men and the way they acted. I just presumed it was him, but now I know it was the secrecy. The hush-hush calls he got, the way he'd look at Jagger, Martin, and Barney whenever he got a call or a text. The meetings they had, nothing was about the club it was all about his business. Mom's words play over in my head. "He's a killer." But she knew that before I got here, she's known for a very long time and yet she let me get close to him, she let me fall in love with him. Why? Why would she do that? I can't wrap my head around this. I don't understand why she thought to tell me now? What would it achieve? All it's done is make me hate them both. The lies, that's all I think, I've been lied to so much, I'm sick of it.

I don't know how long I've been driving for, but when I see the sign for San Leandro, relief washes through me, I'm so close to Oakland. I've not stopped crying since I left Mom's house and it's been hard to see, I honestly can't remember much of the drive. Hopefully I'll be able to have time to reflect, see what to do next. Right now I'm so confused, so hurt that I can't think straight.

My cell ringing has me looking at the screen. Lacey's name flashes, and I answer it. "Hey Lace, you okay?" I say bubbly hoping she won't hear the tears in my voice.

Of course, she doesn't buy it. "Hey Mia, I'm better. Are you?"

"Not really, but I'll tell you some other time." I'm not really ready to tell anyone yet.

"Well tough, I'm in San Fran, well leaving it now, I've got a rental, so I'll be driving up to your mom's house. You can tell me when I get there." She tells me, and I know Lace. She won't stop until she finds out what's wrong.

"Change of plan, I'm going to my old house. I'll give you the address, will you put it into your GPS?"

She doesn't miss a beat, "Sure, tell me what it is." I rattle off the address to her, "Okay, it's saying I'll be there in fifteen minutes."

I smile, "You'll be there before me. There's a gnome in the front yard that has a key in the bottom of it. Let yourself in. I'll be there soon." I tell her, grateful that I have her to vent to when I get there.

"See you soon, Mia." She says and ends the call.

The thirty-minute drive from San Leandro to Oakland doesn't seem that long, my cell has been ringing non-stop since Lacey hung up. Each time it's Mom calling me. Pulling into the driveway, there are two cars parked here. One in the drive beside mine and then one out front. Who else is here?

Shaking my head, I get out of the car and walk toward the front door, surprised that Lacey hasn't come out to me yet. Usually she would. When we're in Arizona, if Lacey and I haven't seen each other in a while we'd always greet each other outside the house.

Pushing the door open, I peer inside the house, it's silent. Where is everyone? Just as I open my mouth to call for them, something flashes in the corner of my eye and as I turn to face it, something connects with my face, pain erupts and I crumple to the floor before blackness takes over.

EIGHTEEN

Hudson

"Boss, what are we going to do?" Aaron asks, his anger is at the forefront as is everyone else's. Not only have Carmine and Jorge been shot, but we've lost three other men. We don't know if they're dead or alive but I'm not holding my breath for them to turn up out of the blue. The one thing I do know is Juan is one hundred percent behind this. That fucker has chosen the wrong man to go to war with.

Looking down at the picture Aaron has just shown me, my teeth bare. "Get me that bitch, and I don't give a fuck what anyone says, she's mine," I tell him and a sinister smile forms on his face. "She's alive when you bring her to me Aaron, if she's not, then you'll face my wrath."

My threat doesn't bother him. "Fuck Boss, you do take away all the fun." He chuckles to himself, "She's yours, but I can't guarantee that she won't be banged up when she gets to you."

I shake my head, "As long as she's alive. Do what you want with her." She's gone too fucking far this time.

"I'll call you when I have her." He promises as he leaves the office.

Fuck, it's always one thing after another. I want to get back to Mia, I've been gone long enough. I'm like a bear around here, my mood is positively pissed every day. She's like a balm, whenever I speak to her my mood lifts for a couple of minutes and then I'm like the devil. Hell, the devil would probably hide from my ornery ass.

My cell rings, "What?" I ask, and if it were anyone other than my men, I wouldn't be surprised if they hung up.

"Son." Dad's voice full of worry has me standing up. "Hudson?"

"Mia? Where is she?" My mind is whirling with every fucking possibility going.

"I don't know son, she left hours ago and we've not heard from her since." He tells me.

"What the fuck, Dad? Hours, she left hours

ago and you're only telling me now?" I yell, wanting to throw the damn cell across the room. "Martin!" I yell needing him in here right now.

"Hudson, Tina and her were talking. They needed to clear the air..." He begins.

"What did she say to make her leave?" I'm barely holding on right now.

"She told her about you."

I close my eyes. "What about me?" My tone clipped.

"Everything, son."

"You let her? What the fuck?" I'm raging right now. He's lucky he's not standing in front of me because I'm pretty sure I'd knock him the hell out.

"I didn't let her. Leave Tina to me, we need to find Mia." He responds, not once raising his voice at me.

The door opens and in walks Martin, his laptop in hand ready for whatever it is I need.

"I'll find her. Keep Tina away from me, Dad. I won't be held responsible for my actions if she's anywhere near me." I end the call.

"Boss, is everything okay?" Martin asks, setting his laptop on my desk.

"No, find Mia and Martin, do it quickly." His

eyes widen at my words, but he nods instantly and gets to work.

My cell rings, and I ignore it, I don't want to talk to anyone, I need to find Mia.

"Okay Boss, I'm pinging her cell as we speak," Martin tells me just as his cell begins to ring. He reaches for it in his pocket and frowns before answering it. "Jag?" He listens to whatever Jagger is saying before handing me his cell.

Sighing, I take it and put it to my ear, "This had better be important." I say through clenched teeth. It must have been him who was calling me.

"Boss, is everything okay?" Whatever the reason he called is now gone, his attention is on me.

I turn my attention to Martin, "Martin, did you find Mia?"

"Shit. What's happened?"

I ignore Jagger and focus on Martin, "Boss, her cell is in Oakland." He tells me the address, and it's one that I know. It's where she used to live when she was growing up. "Boss, what do we do?"

"Hear that?" I ask Jagger as my feet move toward the door.

"Yes, I'm getting in the car now. What's happened?" He asks again.

“Tina told her about me, and what I do. She’s been gone for hours.”

"Fuck." He says through clenched teeth, “I’m leaving now.”

"I'll meet you at the house," I tell him and end the call. "Martin, you coming?" I call out as I continue to walk toward the exit of the club.

He catches up to me as I reach the car, "I'm driving." I tell him opening the driver's side. "Get in."

He does as I say and I put the car in drive and put my foot down. "Hudson, want to tell me what's happened?" Martin asks.

"Tina and my dad got home last night," I say through clenched teeth, my knuckles white as I grip the steering wheel. "Tina decided to have a talk with Mia, which was needed but then she decided she'd tell Mia everything about me."

"Shit, what did she think she was going to accomplish by telling her that?" Martin sounds pissed, he knows what Mia means to me and having someone else tell her about me and what I do for a living means that she'll think I'm a liar.

"Call Barney and put him on speaker," I tell him, I want to know why she was allowed to leave the house.

"On it Boss." He replies, and the sound of the dial tone hits my ears.

"Martin, is everything okay?" Barney asks as he answers the phone.

"Where are you?" I growl, pissed that he allowed her to leave the house.

"Boss?" He questions.

"I asked you a question. Where are you?"

"I'm at home. Your dad told me to go home, get some rest. That he had it covered from there. Why, what's happened?" He's on edge now.

Fucking Dad. "Mia's gone. Tina told her about me, everything about me, and Mia fled back to Oakland."

"Shit, do you need me to help search?"

My anger toward him has diminished. "No, get in contact with Aaron and ask him if he needs assistance."

"On it, call if you need me." He tells me and ends the call just as we pass the Welcome to Oakland sign.

I'm pulling up outside Mia's house within five minutes, and I immediately notice two cars parked here, both parked in the drive. As I get out of the car Jagger's truck pulls up behind my car. He's out of it within seconds.

"She here?" He asks.

"I don't know, her car's here, I've not been inside yet," I reply and start walking toward the house. As I get closer, I notice the front door is ajar. "Fuck," I bite out as I reach for my gun at my back.

Walking to the front door, Martin walks in front of me, and I roll my eyes, he always makes sure that he's in front in case we're ambushed. His foot nudges the door open, his gun raised high as he glances around the house. I immediately still as I see blood on the floor. Jagger pushes past me and into the house, Martin is checking each room as I glance back at the blood. It's at the door, what the hell happened to make someone bleed here? Is it Mia's blood? Glancing up, my gaze hits a set of luggage, frowning I walk over to it, looking at the tag, it has the name Lacey Kane on it.

"Boss." The low tone of Jagger's voice has my blood running cold. Walking over to him, he's looking at the floor, Following his gaze I spot the pool of blood. Whoever the hell bled, needs to get medical help and quickly.

"Boss, she's not here," Martin tells me. All I see is a haze of red.

"She's gone?" Jagger whispers his eyes on me.

"Boss…" Martin begins.

"No, no 'Boss'. Lacey and Mia are gone." I tell him. "I don't care what's going on; someone has my woman, the love of my life. I want her back. I want both of them back, and whoever took them I want their head on a fucking platter. Do I make myself clear?" I ask not bothering looking at Jagger.

He nods, "I'll get every man, woman, and child on it now."

"Call Barney, tell him that he and Aaron need to find that bitch. This shit has Juan written all over it." He turns and leaves, leaving Jagger and me alone.

"Hudson..." Jagger's voice is strong. This is why he's my right-hand man.

"Don't!" I growl, my emotions are on the surface. "Just don't. I'm going to find her Jag, and I'm going to make this city bleed until I do."

He stands up taller, his expression going from worry to anger. "I'm going to kill whoever has her."

I smile, that's the Jagger I know. "There's one person to start with...." He frowns and I smirk. "Got a picture today, Jag, your ex has moved on to Juan. If I find out she had anything to do with this, nothing, and I mean nothing is going to stop me from taking her life."

His eyes flash, "If she orchestrated this, I'll help."

I nod, "It's time to make this city realize what happens when you take someone I love."

Jagger smiles as we leave the house. "Shit, this city is fucked."

I shrug, I don't give a fuck. "Don't take what's mine."

I get into my car and put it in drive. It's time to call in a couple of markers.

The End…

For Now …

Available for Pre-order

Dangerous Secrets

More of The Kingpin Series

Want part 2?

Dangerous Secrets
The Kingpin part 2

Sometimes the enemies closer to home are the ones you have to watch out for.

Hudson's world is rocked on its axis when Mia is kidnapped.

With a list of enemies a mile long, and barely any clues off where to start, Hudson's got to figure out who's brazen enough to take the one he loves.

As secrets are exposed and lies come to the surface, there's only one thing that is certain: Hudson will go to any lengths to have her safe in his arms again.

Will he be able to find Mia before the time runs out or will the Kingpin bathe the streets with blood in vain?

Available for Pre-order

Dangerous Secrets

Are You Following Brooke?

All the ways you can follow Brooke.

Website: https://brookesummer-sautho.wixsite.com/website
Newsletter: http://eepurl.com/gC1j8P
Facebook:
https://www.facebook.com/BrookeSummersAuthor/
Join Brooke's Babes: https://www.facebook.com/groups/BrookesBabes/
Bookbub: https://www.bookbub.com/authors/brooke-summers
Instagram:
https://www.instagram.com/author_brookesummers/
Twitter: https://twitter.com/Author_BrookeS

Acknowledgments

Yashira: Thank you so much for all of your help and hard work, you're amazing and I'm so grateful to have you in my life.

Tiffany: I can't thank you enough for everything you've done to help me. You're a star!

Jen: Ah, you're fabulous! Thank you!

Krissy: Thank you for not only beta reading this but formatting it too. Love you muchly.

Wendy: Thank you. I love you.

Sarah, Dawn, Rachel, Yashira, and Krissy. Thank

you all so much for reading Forbidden Lust and helping me make it into the book it is today.

And thank you to you, for reading this book. Hope you enjoyed it and can't wait for the next one in the series.

Lots of Love

Brooke

Made in USA - North Chelmsford, MA
1327381_9781656149947
08.16.2022 1430